"I wish I hadn't started this personal conversation."

"I think it's a fine conversation," Sam said.

"It's not the kind that should go on between employer and employee," Sally insisted.

"That's true, but we aren't employer and employee now. Tonight we're simply dinner dates. But I'll change the subject for you—I'll explain why I kissed you."

Sally suddenly felt her face turn red. She could barely breathe.

"I kissed you for a lot of reasons. Because you're terrific looking, because I felt like it, because I wanted to see if there was anything impulsive about you—if you could do anything spur-of-the-moment. If you could take a risk. And," he whispered, "it proved something. You can. And very well indeed..."

Dear Reader,

Though it may be cold outside during the month of November, it's always warmed by the promise of the upcoming holiday season. What better time to curl up with a good book? What better time for Silhouette Romance?

And in November, we've got some wonderful books to take the chill off these cold winter months. Continuing our DIAMOND JUBILEE celebration is *Song of the Lorelei*, by Lucy Gordon. Escape to the romantic world of brooding Conrad von Feldstein. The haunting secret at von Feldstein Castle is revealed when beautiful Laurel Blake pays a visit . . . and love finally comes home. Don't miss this emotional, poignant tale!

The DIAMOND JUBILEE—Silhouette Romance's tenth anniversary celebration—is our way of saying thanks to you, our readers. To symbolize the timelessness of love, as well as the modern gift of the tenth anniversary, we're presenting readers with a DIAMOND JUBILEE Silhouette Romance each month, penned by one of your favorite Silhouette Romance authors. And rounding up the year, next month be sure to watch for *Only the Nanny Knows for Sure*, by Phyllis Halldorson.

And that's not all! There are six books a month from Silhouette Romance—stories by wonderful writers who, time and time again, bring home the magic of love. During our anniversary year, each book is special and written with romance in mind. This month, and in the future, work by such loved writers as Diana Palmer, Brittany Young and Annette Broadrick is sure to put a smile on your face.

During our tenth anniversary, the spirit of celebration is with us year-round. And that's all due to you, our readers. With the support you've given to us, you can look forward to many more years of heartwarming, poignant love stories.

I hope you'll enjoy this book and all of the stories to come. Come home to romance—Silhouette Romance—for always!

Sincerely,
Tara Hughes Gavin
Senior Editor

OCTAVIA STREET

A Question of Risk

Silhouette Romance

Published by Silhouette Books New York

America's Publisher of Contemporary Romance

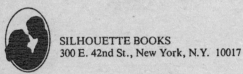

SILHOUETTE BOOKS
300 E. 42nd St., New York, N.Y. 10017

ISBN: 0-373-08758-6

First Silhouette Books printing November 1990

Printed in the U.S.A.

Books by Octavia Street

Silhouette Romance

Words of Love #582
November Returns #612
Red Sky at Night #680
A Question of Risk #758

OCTAVIA STREET

grew up in Colorado and Montana. She now lives in San Francisco and travels often. She writes nonfiction in addition to romances. She recently received a Lifetime Achievement Award for ruthlessly cleaning out the garage.

ENGLAND AND SCOTLAND

N

SCOTLAND

Aberdeen

Dundee

Edinburgh

Glasgow

HOLY ISLAND

North Sea

Irish Sea

Manchester

Birmingham

WALES

ENGLAND

London

English Channel

FRANCE

Chapter One

The letter was written on ecru stationery with an embossed floral design at the top.

> Dearest Sam,
> I cannot sleep nights thinking of you. You are in my mind night and day. I am a tall, beautiful blonde, and I would like to get to know you. I would like to start by giving you a ride in my Lamborghini. That is only the beginning. I will do anything for you. My phone number is 555-9760. I am ready and waiting.
>
> Gloria T.

Over the signature was a lipstick kiss.

Sally Forbes looked at this missive with astonishment and said to Sam Thatcher's secretary, "Marcy, are you supposed to be opening his personal mail? That's terrible!"

"Oh, he gets these things all the time," Marcy said. "He doesn't pay any attention to them, but we pass them around the office and laugh. We call them mash notes. This one is mild. Some of them ask for money, others make really indecent suggestions."

Sally was amazed. "Mr. Thatcher gets a lot of these?" She had seen her new employer only once, for about fifteen seconds, and he hadn't seemed to her the type who would attract mash notes from women with Lamborghinis. Not that he was ugly or anything. He was quite nice looking, but very conservative. Gray suit, white shirt, subdued tie, that sort of thing. He faded into the background. Even his offices were conservative, decently furnished, well decorated, but eminently forgettable. It was a kind of generic office for a kind of generic man.

Marcy said, "Ever since his picture appeared on the cover of *Fortune* magazine, these letters started coming in. Then there was the big write-up in the *Wall Street Journal*. And there are phone calls. I don't understand it either."

"That's astonishing," Sally said. "What did the article in the *Journal* say? What did *Fortune* say that set the women off?"

"Nothing," said Marcy. "At least nothing that I could see that would cause it. Both of them called him an authentic genius, but I never heard of Einstein getting mash notes. I thought it only happened to rock stars."

"Is there a copy of *Fortune* around here?" Sally asked.

"No. It's banned. He won't allow it around. He's sorry he let them do the article."

"Why? Because of the letters?" Sally asked.

"That's part of it. Plus he already had more business than he could handle, and those articles just caused the telephone to ring off the hook."

"Is he married?" Sally asked, looking again at the mash note.

"No, he's not married," March said. "And pity the poor woman who tries it. You'll find out. An authentic genius is like an opera star, or something. A whirlwind. The only reason there's any breathing space around here now is that he's in Kuala Lumpur. When he comes back in that door, duck. Things will start flying around. It's like living in a tornado."

"Marcy, how long have you been working here?" Sally asked.

"Two years, and I've just about reached the end of my rope. He's really nice, really generous, but he's impossible to keep up with. I have to do all kinds of things that are against my principles—like take his suits to the cleaner's. In this day and age, secretaries don't do that. You'll find out what it's like—just wait."

"Remember, I'm only a temp," Sally said, smiling. "I'm here to set up the books and do the taxes, after what that so-called bookkeeper of yours did. That's all. I won't have to take his suits to the cleaner's. I just do my job and go on to some other place. So I'll survive it."

"Well, we've got a few days to relax before he gets back," Marcy told her. "Is there anything you need?"

Sally had forgotten what it was she had come to Marcy's desk to ask for. Then she remembered. "Where's the computer paper kept?"

"The supply room," said Marcy. "Here, I'll show you."

"Well, how was your first day at Sam Thatcher's?" asked Sally's friend Alicia, over drinks at Beau Geste.

Beau Geste was full of ferns and fake Tiffany glass and old mirrors advertising breweries gone out of business a hundred years before. Sally and Alicia made it a point to meet somewhere for drinks or dinner at least once a week. They had been friends since grade school.

"My first day was strange," said Sally. "The man is making a fortune and is trying to run his business out of his checkbook. The bookkeeper must have been addicted to something. I never saw anything like it. Those accounts are hopeless."

"That's not what I mean, Sally. What's Sam Thatcher like? From his pictures, he looks like a real hunk."

"Sam Thatcher isn't even in the country. I saw him for about ten seconds last week when I went over to talk about taking the job. He just kind of waved at me. His book-keeper walked out and left the books looking like the Chinese army had marched through them. He had to get a CPA in fast and get his books in order, and I was the CPA. So that's all he saw: three letters. And all I saw was a man in a suit. He may be a hunk, but you couldn't prove it by me."

Alicia sighed. "Sally Forbes, you've been Miss Oblivious ever since I've known you. You were the only one in our high school class who didn't recognize Leo Coyote at the reunion." Leo Coyote, once Leonard Smith, undersized sophomore, had become a world-famous rock star. Sally still couldn't remember him, even after being shown his picture in the yearbook.

"Alicia, that was more than ten years ago. And I'm not a rock fan, you know that. And anyway, you said yourself he had plastic surgery," Sally said, sipping her white wine. Then, to distract Alicia, she asked, "How's everything at Woolfe and Fisher? How's George?"

Alicia was a fashion buyer at Woolfe and Fisher, a de-partment store, and George was her long-time boyfriend. Alicia had been talking about quitting the store and about marrying George for the past eight years. She admitted she couldn't bring herself to do either.

"The store is boring. George is boring," Alicia said wryly. "Maybe I'll get lucky, like you, and the store will fail and I'll lose my job."

"I was lucky?" Sally said with a laugh. "How could Metropolitan failing be lucky for me?"

"Didn't you just tell me you liked working temporary jobs better? It's been two years, and I've never seen you happier."

"It's true that I make more money and have more time off, and the work is more interesting," Sally said. "But I'm still not used to it. I'm not a temporary kind of person. I'm the kind of person who needs a steady job."

"Well, you do have a steady job. It's just not at the same place all the time."

Sally sighed. "I like predictability. I like routine."

"Sally, you're hopeless," said Alicia. "At least you've said your jobs were fun, right?"

"Except this job. This one may not be so much fun. It really is a mess, and I'm afraid that Mr. Sam Thatcher, the cover boy, probably owes the Internal Revenue a whole bunch of money. He's not going to be happy about it. And I'll be the one who has to tell him."

"While you're handing him the tax bill, take a good look at him, okay?" Alicia said.

"Okay," Sally said, tossing a lock of long black hair out of her eyes. "I'll take a good look, and then I'll run."

As it happened, the tornado arrived in Sam Thatcher's office two days before he did. A letter came from the Internal Revenue Service, telling him to bring his records and his accountant and come down for a little discussion of his business and personal taxes from four years before. Sally had read the letter and groaned. She had not even managed to get this year's taxes straightened out, much less those from four years ago.

The morning of Sam Thatcher's return from Kuala Lumpur, Sally took extra special care with her appearance. She wore a new gray suit, with a lavender sweater under it which made her eyes a deep violet. She brushed her shoulder-length black hair until it shone. In winter, her skin became very pale, so she put on just the faintest touch of blush over what Alicia called good bone structure, and what Sally thought of as her American Indian cheekbones.

Just before she stepped out the door to catch her bus, she gave herself a farewell glance in the mirror. For today was the day that she had to tell her employer, a man she had never *really* met, that he owed Internal Revenue at least $20,000, plus penalties and interest, and that was just the beginning. She was grateful that she was, after all, a temporary employee and could easily go on to another job. She knew the nature of employers: upon hearing bad tidings, they tended to shoot the messenger. Therefore, she always tried to look her best on the days she was likely to be fired—a superstition, of course, but at least it made her feel better.

She arrived promptly at nine and had been bent over the computer with its Lotus 1-2-3 program for half an hour before Sam Thatcher came in. Sally had appropriated an empty office and had papers and printouts spread around on whatever piece of furniture was available. She could not see the reception area. But she heard him arrive, heard him greet Marcy, heard him go into his office, heard the door close. One of the lights on the phone went on instantly and stayed on for quite a while.

Sally began to fidget. She had worked it out with Marcy the day before: Sally would let him get settled in, then she would just go in and face him down with it. Marcy had been far less worried than she was. "Don't worry," Marcy had said. "He's never thrown anyone out a window yet. I'll tell him you want to see him."

The light went out on the phone. Sally heard the door open, heard someone moving around, greeting various people, heard footsteps approach her door.

A head came around the corner. "Hi," it said. "Who are you?"

"I'm Sally Forbes," she said. "The CPA."

But the head had disappeared before she could even finish.

And that was her second glimpse of Sam Thatcher.

It was nearly five in the afternoon before Sally, armed with the IRS letter and several file folders, finally marched into the office of the authentic genius. By this time, after five attempts to see him, she had concluded that Sam Thatcher was like the absentminded professor who wound up the cat and put the alarm clock out. That had a certain charm, she supposed, but the IRS was notoriously unsusceptible to charm. Somebody had to put a stop to it—the alarm had gone off.

Sam Thatcher was sitting behind his desk, his suit coat off, writing on a legal pad. As Sally walked in he looked up and said, "Hello," in a tone of voice that made Sally realize that he had no idea who she was.

Sally went straight to his desk and put her file folders on it. "I'm Sally Forbes. I'm the CPA that Acme Temporaries sent over and I've been working on your books. There's a serious problem that you must do something about immediately."

Sam Thatcher was leaning forward, looking at her with narrowed eyes. "What's that?" he asked.

k in the narrowed eyes and the aggressive pos-
the big desk. She flinched only slightly and bit
wn hard on the bullet. "Well, for starters, Internal Revenue says you owe them $20,000, plus penalties and interest
from four years ago. And as far as I can tell, they're right.
And that's just for starters."

"Amazing," said Sam Thatcher mildly.

"What's amazing?" asked Sally. "The IRS?"

"I never saw anyone with black hair and purple eyes before."

Sally realized that her jaw had dropped. There was a long
silence in the room, and she stood stiffly in front of his desk
while Sam Thatcher looked up at her and smiled. That was
when she realized that he wasn't ordinary looking at all. He
was, in fact, a hunk. Ordinary brown hair, brown eyes, to
be sure, but good craggy features set in a square face. He
had a strong chin, a slightly crooked nose that anyone would
recognize as being broken once, and under the conservative
white shirt and foulard tie was a long lean body that
wouldn't stop. To match the slightly crooked nose there was
a slightly crooked grin.

Finally Sally said, "Huh?"

"I said I never saw anyone with black hair and purple eyes
before. That's really spectacular," he said, "Now, have a
seat and tell me about this $20,000, or whatever it is." He
gestured at a chair in front of his desk.

Weak-kneed with astonishment, Sally dropped into the
chair and reached over and opened the folder with the letter from the IRS on top. "They're giving you thirty days,"
she said, "and I can't even begin to get everything together
in thirty days. It's those foreign tax credits. You need a team
of accountants. And you'll probably need a tax lawyer after that."

Sam Thatcher said, "Okay. Hire a team of accountants. Hire a tax lawyer. Get it straightened out. That's what you're here for."

"But—" Sally began.

"Do you like zinfandel?" he asked.

"Do I like zinfandel?" Sally echoed.

"Zinfandel, the wine?" he said, as if Sally were a first-grader.

"Oh," she said.

"I'm a little jet-lagged," said Sam Thatcher. "And happy hour approaches. Want to go to the Hoffmeister's?"

"Hoffmeister's?" echoed Sally again.

"Are you new in town?" he asked, putting on his suit coat. "Never heard of zinfandel or Hoffmeister's? Well, no matter. Get your coat."

"Tin," said Sam Thatcher. "The whole problem's tin. So when the United States dumped its strategic reserve, the bottom dropped out of the tin market, and Malaysia nearly went under. Malaysia was trying to diversify, but still, tin was nearly thirty percent of the gross domestic product. So the Hong Kong and Shanghai Bank decided to form a consortium...am I boring you?" He looked across the table at Sally with a quizzical expression.

Sally, who had made the mistake of asking him what he had been doing in Kuala Lumpur, shook her head. She had followed most of what he had said, but her attention had been on the man himself. She wondered how she could have thought he was a nonentity. There he was, telling her all about Malaysia, right across the table from her, in crowded noisy Hoffmeister's, where they were now eating dinner, and all she could do was stare idiotically at first one of his features and then another.

As he talked about the new car being built in partnership
with Mitsubishi at Kelang, she had studied his eyebrows,
deciding that they were very expressive. Relations with Singapore had given her the opportunity to notice his chin and
then the widow's peak. His disquisition on tin had caused
her to watch his hands, which were big, strong and remark-
ably graceful and quick for a man his size. She was still half-
hypnotized when she realized that he had stopped talking
and was staring at her.

"Where did you get that coloring?" he asked. "That
black hair and that fair skin and those purple eyes. Amazing."

Sally was much more accustomed to employers who noticed her cash management abilities, or her knowledge of the
tax advantages of LIFO versus FIFO. First she felt self-
conscious, and then felt herself begin to blush. Sally Forbes
hadn't blushed since junior high school.

"I inherited it," she stammered. "My father is mostly
English descent and my mother is half American Indian. I
can't help it."

"Yes," he said studying her face. "I can see the Indian
cheekbones, now. Which tribe?"

"Blackfeet."

"Where's that?"

"Montana," Sally said, relieved that he was diverted from
staring directly into her eyes, purple or not.

"Are you from Montana?" he asked.

"No. My mother was. I was born here."

"And you are a Certified Public Accountant and an
American Indian with purple eyes." He grinned a crooked
grin across the table at her. Sally decided she was about to
drown in his eyes, in that smile. She looked at the hunting
print on the wall behind him and made a desperate attempt

to flounder out of the deep water into which she was sinking.

"Can we try another word besides purple? It makes me think of eggplant," Sally said, trying to sound businesslike and disapproving. "And do you mind if we discuss your tax problem, instead of my ancestry?"

"Decide what you want for dessert, first." he said. "While I think of synonyms for purple. I'm not very good with colors. It was meant as a compliment."

"I don't care for dessert, thanks. And I know you meant it as a compliment. But I'm not kidding about your taxes. And neither is the IRS." Sally said this sternly.

"I'm sure they aren't," he said. "And I'm sure you aren't. And it's something I've neglected, and you came in to straighten it out. You say you need a team of accountants—fine, hire a team. I should have done it long ago, but it's been very busy out there, since the Third World debt crisis. That's a pretty lame excuse for the IRS, but I'm sure they'll gladly take my money, anyway. I'll sign the checks. But don't bother me with the details. I don't know anything about making a lot of money. You can hire people to do the things you don't like to do."

"True," said Sally. "But what is it you want me to do?"

"Whatever is necessary," he said. "Are you good at what you do? Are you a good CPA?"

"Of course I am. And I know the Internal Revenue Code inside out. I worked in the tax department of Metropolitan—"

But Sam interrupted. "Then you've got carte blanche. And double your salary. Starting tomorrow. Tonight, I want to have a brandy and then get a good night's sleep. I spent all day yesterday on a plane. I don't want to talk about taxes."

"Then why are we here?" Sally asked.

"Because I never saw anybody with purple eyes and black hair before," said Sam Thatcher, as if that were the most obvious statement in the world.

A few days later, Sally and Alicia had decided to have their weekly dinner at Sally's apartment. Sally had bought a food processor and wanted to try it out on Alicia before she got serious and had real company over.

After the vichyssoise Alicia said, "So what happened after that? He said he didn't want to talk about taxes, and you said...?"

Sally was helping herself to the diced lamb curry with mango chutney. "I didn't say much of anything. He sent me home in a taxi. I haven't spoken to him since. I've seen him going in and out."

"Pass the Julienned beets," Alicia said. "They're really good. So did you hire a team of accountants and a tax lawyer?"

Sally shook her head. "I decided he didn't need the tax lawyer yet, but I called Acme and they sent over two bookkeeper types, and we are starting to get the thing under control."

"I'll have the last of the pureed squash, too," said Alicia. "I think it's great that you finally opened your eyes and took a look. He is a hunk, isn't he?"

"You were right. He is a hunk. And he's got a girlfriend, too. I kept my eyes open a little longer and saw her coming in, and saw them go out together."

"What does she look like?" Alicia asked, reaching for the diced apple and celery salad.

"Well, she's blond and she looks a lot like..." Sally stopped to think.

"Bette Midler, I hope?" said Alicia.

"More like Faye Dunaway. That rich, sleek, sophisticated type."

"Pity. Otherwise you might have had a chance."

"Cut it out, Alicia," Sally said. "The man is my employer. Just because he's a hunk doesn't mean I have any kind of interest in him other than financial." She was not about to confess that she had sat across from him at Hoffmeister's and let her imagination run wild.

"What does he do to make all this money that he owes taxes on?" Alicia took some of the zucchini stuffed with pureed carrots and potatoes.

"He's an international consultant," Sally said.

"Well, that's nice and vague. What does that mean?"

"I'm not exactly sure. It says 'Country Risk Analyst' on his stationery. And you wouldn't believe the accounts receivable—big banks, multinationals, oil companies, the World Bank, even governments."

"Country risk analyst?" Alicia said. "I'll bet I know what that is. If you go to Honduras and drink the water you risk . . ."

"I don't think that's quite the idea," Sally told her, spooning up some pureed beets. "I know he puts out some kind of newsletter. I've seen it floating around. And there are people around the office working at computers."

"Well, I know how to find out what he does. Get a copy of that *Fortune* magazine."

"I can't imagine where," Sally said. "He won't allow it in the office. Here, have some applesauce."

"You can get it at the public library," Alicia said smugly. "I'm about three blocks from the main branch. I can get it on my lunch hour."

"If you want to waste your lunch hour, that's fine with me," said Sally. "Now, would you like some coffee?"

"As long as you didn't put it through that food processor," Alicia told her. "I couldn't take pureed coffee."

Chapter Two

Today there were more mash notes in the mail. "Listen to this," said Marcy. "'I dream of you at night. I wear my pink silk nightgown and sleep on ivory satin sheets. Please send money.'"

She picked up another. "This is typical, too. 'I am a beautiful lingerie model, age 25. I do not drink or smoke and I go to church every Sunday. But on Saturday...' Just as soon as the letters die down, something happens to set them off again."

"What was it this time?" Sally asked.

"Oh, he was on local TV. An ambush interview," Marcy said.

"I missed that," Sally said. "Probably the only chance I would ever have of seeing him again. Marcy, I've got to talk to him. I've talked to the IRS auditor all I can. Now, it's his turn."

Marcy looked sympathetic. "I understand. But I can't do anything about it. Maybe when he gets in from New Orleans." She looked at her desk calendar. "In about an hour, if the plane's on time."

"I didn't even know he was out of town," Sally said in exasperation. "How can I poss—"

"Oh, lord," interrupted Marcy. "I forgot his suits. I forgot to take them to the cleaners." She jumped up from her desk. "Wanna come with me? Want to see where he lives? It'll only take a few minutes."

Sally started to say no, and then she decided she did want to see where he lived. It was pure nosiness, of course, but she imagined he had some kind of fabulous bachelor pad. She would never see it any other way.

So, she was very surprised when Marcy simply walked across the street and went into the hotel opposite the office building. Sally followed Marcy to the elevator, where Marcy punched the button marked "10." Certainly he had one of the suites, she assumed, as she followed Marcy down the hushed corridor. Marcy opened one of the doors with a key and ushered Sally in.

"He lives in one hotel room?" Sally asked in astonishment.

"One hotel room," Marcy said, going to the closet.

And that was exactly what it was, although a large one. And it looked exactly like a hotel room. There were hardly any personal things around, just a few books, some loose change on the dresser, and two *Wall Street Journal*s in plastic wrappers on a chair by the door.

Sally was gaping.

Marcy was pulling an armload of suits out of the closet. "It does make sense," she told Sally. "He's gone three weeks out of every month."

"What a life," Sally said. "Does he do anything but work?"

"I don't think so," Marcy told her. "Not here, anyway. For all I know, though, he could be lying on a beach in Tahiti when he's out of the country. Maybe this time he went to New Orleans for Mardi Gras."

"I don't think it's Mardi Gras time," Sally said. "Here, let me help you with some of those suits."

A husky voice at the door said, "It isn't Mardi Gras in New Orleans. It was last month."

Both Sally and Marcy jumped.

Sam Thatcher walked into the room and dropped a battered leather suitcase on the bed. "Hi, Marcy," he said with a smile. There was a short pause, and he added, "Uh, nice to see you again, uh, Sally, isn't it?"

Sally nodded. She supposed she should be flattered that he remembered her name. She also supposed that she should be embarrassed at being caught flagrantly in his "home" or worse, his bedroom, but he didn't seem to mind. He was, in fact, taking some papers out of the suitcase and putting them in an attaché case, paying absolutely no attention to her or to Marcy.

"Ready?" he said, straightening. He ushered them out the door, Marcy carrying her load of suits. She dropped a vest in the corridor, and Sally, walking behind, picked it up and carried it for her.

At the front door of the hotel, Marcy said, "I'll see you in the office," took the vest from Sally and went off down the street. As Sam and Sally and a hundred others waited for the light to change, Sally realized that this might be her only chance to talk to Sam Thatcher for weeks.

"I've got to talk to you," she said, close to desperation. "The Internal Revenue—"

"Want to buy a Rolex for a hundred dollars?" said a voice, and Sally saw a dapper man standing in front of her holding an open attaché case full of watches.

Others waiting at the curb crowded in to look.

"Real Rolex," said the man, dangling one in front of Sam's nose. "Can't tell you where they came from, but it had to do with customs at the airport."

"No, thanks," Sam said politely. "But let me see that a minute." He quickly took the watch from the man's hand.

The light changed to green and the Walk light came on, but no one moved. Everyone on the corner was watching Sam. As the watch-seller objected, Sam pried open the back and shook out the watch works. "Just as I thought," he said. "Case made in Taiwan, works made in Hong Kong. Probably assembled there. It's worth about twenty bucks retail."

Then he handed the watch and the works back to the would-be seller and walked across the street on the flashing Don't Walk light, with Sally trotting behind. Was that what country risk experts did? she wondered. She caught up with him at the door of the office building and followed him into the elevator.

"I've got to talk to you," she began again. "The Internal—"

But just as he pushed the button for the fortieth floor, and the doors began to glide shut, a woman dashed into the elevator.

"Sam, I've got to talk to you," the woman said.

"That's my line," said Sally under her breath. Then she took a second look at the woman and realized it was the tall cool sophisticated blonde who she had seen in the office, the one who looked like Faye Dunaway. It was the woman she had assumed was his girlfriend.

But Sam wasn't acting as if she was his girlfriend. He didn't seem to be glad to see her. She had backed him up into the corner of the elevator and was saying something to him in a low voice. Sally was trying very hard not to listen.

Or at least to look as if she wasn't listening. She had her back resolutely turned.

She paid careful attention to the numbers above the door. This was an express elevator, and the numbers started at "20." When "30" lit up, Sally heard Sam say, "There's somebody I'd like you to meet." And she felt a hand on her arm.

The hand was pulling her around until she found herself standing next to Sam, face to face with the blonde. The hand, in fact, was gripping her arm so tightly that her circulation was cut off.

"This is Sally," Sam said. "We're getting married as soon as we can make the arrangements. Sally's very jealous. She wouldn't like it at all if I went off with you in your Lamborghini."

Fortunately, the blonde was looking at Sam and not Sally, because Sally's mouth opened, and a strange sound started to come out, but it was cut short by more pressure from the hand gripping her arm. She covered it with a cough. Just then there was a ping as the elevator swooped to a stop and the doors opened.

Sam steered Sally out, reached in and punched the Lobby button and stepped back. The doors closed on the irate looking blonde, and Sally watched the numbers light up in descending order in the brass plate above the elevator. Her mouth was still open, and she was rubbing her arm where Sam had gripped it.

"I apologize for that," he said. "But it was the only way I could think of to get rid of her. She lies in wait for me."

"Any time," said Sally, ironically. "Happy to be of use."

He held open the outer door of the office, and as she went through, Sally said, "I really do have to talk to you. The Internal Revenue..."

"Later," Sam said, heading for his office. "I have some phone calls to make."

Of course, she didn't see him again that week.

Sunday was Sally's favorite day. She had developed a ritual over the years. All week long she was compulsively, terribly organized, something that came naturally to her. She was well aware that her profession of accounting was closely related to her basic personality and that, in turn, was due to her painful family background. But there was another side to Sally, and on Sundays it blossomed.

Sunday was her own day, her day to do the things that satisfied her very soul. She was, underneath the CPA, a nest-maker. She loved her apartment. Sundays were to be domestic, to do needlepoint or quilting, or some other project. She loved to cook, and Sunday evenings she often invited a friend or friends to dinner. If she did not invite someone over, she practiced on a difficult new dish herself.

Someone had given her a Moroccan cookbook, and she had decided to try making couscous for herself before she tried it on somebody else. She had just started to put in the cinnamon and the saffron—which she had scoured the city for—when the doorbell rang.

Muttering under her breath, she headed for the door and looked through the peephole. She could see nothing but a sweater—whoever it was, was tall. Leaving the chain on, she opened the door a few inches and peered out.

Sam Thatcher was standing outside her door.

Sally stared for a moment in frozen amazement and then shut the door and took the chain off. It was a number of seconds before she remembered to open the door again.

Sam Thatcher said, "May I come in?" and without waiting for a reply, he walked past her into the apartment.

He looked around at the carefully selected antiques, the Isfahan rug, the devotedly nurtured plants, the excellent prints, the big pillowy off-white couch, and he said, "Wow. I like this."

Sally, still standing at the open door, was torn between astonishment that he was here at all, and irritation that he—or anyone—would walk in uninvited and pass judgment, good or bad, on her home. On her special and private place that she had worked so hard to get just the way she wanted it.

She opened her mouth to say something tart, but Sam cut her off with, "You said you wanted to talk to me, so I thought I'd drop by."

"I...I..." Sally floundered, but Sam suddenly said in a different tone of voice, "Now they're green. How did you manage that?"

"How did I manage what?" she said.

"Last time I looked you had purple eyes. Now they're green," he said.

"It's because they match whatever I wear, and I have on, you may have noticed, this icky green sweatshirt. Therefore, I have icky green eyes."

"Ah so," said Sam. "Don't you think you ought to close the door?"

Though seriously tempted to close it with Sam on the other side, Sally swung the door shut. Then she said, "How did you find out where I live?"

"Phone book," he said.

"I'm not listed," she told him.

"Well, actually, I remembered the address you gave the taxi driver, the time we went to Hoffmeister's."

Sally said, "How could you possibly remember my address, when I know you have trouble remembering my name?"

"I'm terrible with names," he said. "But I never forget a number." He paused a moment, and then said conversationally, "What's burning?"

As Sally sniffed and looked up at the ceiling to see a thin film of gray smoke curling out of the kitchen, the smoke alarm went off. She dashed past Sam into the kitchen to see a red hot frying pan full of onions and raisins and butter and ginger and cinnamon and sugar and about five dollars worth of saffron erupting smoke like Mount Saint Helens.

"Allow me," said Sam, who had followed her. He picked up the pan, put it in the sink and turned on the water. There were ominous snapping sounds. Through clouds of steam, he reached up and disabled the squealing smoke alarm and then opened the window. Sally, meanwhile, turned off the offending burner and was looking dejectedly at what remained of her grand couscous experiment.

"Damn it," she said. She started to add, "It's all your fault," but Sam interrupted her.

"That's okay," he told her. "It's all my fault. I'll help you clean it up. Do you like pizza?"

Sally gulped and said, "Yes."

"Why don't we just send out for pizza, instead. My treat."

So, in less than half an hour, Sally found herself on the rug in front of the fireplace, basking in front of a roaring fire, and eating slices of pizza with everything including anchovies. All of this had been brought about by Sam seemingly without effort. He treated her apartment as if it were his. He was completely at ease. And this had made Sally even more tense.

"Great pizza, don't you think?" Sam said.

"Yes. Why did you do this?"

"Do what?" asked Sam, leaning back on one elbow.

"Come over, order pizza, the whole thing."

"To tell you the truth, I wanted to see where you lived," Sam said. "And I couldn't think of a very good excuse, so I just came over. And I owe you the pizza, at least."

"Do you do that with all your employees?" Sally asked.

"No," said Sam. "Just you."

"Why did you want to see where I lived?"

"Because it's a good way to tell a lot about a person, don't you think?"

"Uh, yes," said Sally, her head spinning from trying to follow his logic. Something was missing.

Then Sam said, "Why don't you tell me about you."

Sally glanced over and saw that he was looking full at her.

"I'm not a good subject of conversation," she said.

"You look good to me."

"Please," Sally said, with a little too much emotion, "Let's talk about something else."

"I want to talk about you," Sam said. "It's easy. All you have to do is answer a few questions."

"What kind of questions?" Sally asked warily.

"Oh, like: What's your favorite disease?"

Sally choked on her beer, coughing and laughing at the same time. She shook her head, unable to speak.

"Obviously, you didn't like that one. I'll try another. What's the capital of Sri Lanka?"

"Bismark," said Sally.

"That's the capital of North Dakota."

"Well, I was close."

"What's your favorite ice-cream flavor?"

"Bubble gum mocha."

"Mine, too. What a coincidence. See how easy it is to talk about yourself?" Sam said with a crooked grin. "Your turn."

"Okay," said Sally. "What do you think about the windfall profits tax?"

"I never think about it," he said. "Not a fair question."

"What's a fair question?"

"What's your favorite movie?"

"*Tootsie*. No. *The Gods Must Be Crazy*."

"Mine's the *Pink Panther* movies."

"I take it back. I love the *Pink Panther* movies."

"I need a phooone in thees hotel rheum," said Sam.

"You sound just like Inspector Clouseau."

"Remember the scene where Cato the houseboy jumps out of the refrigerator?" Sam began laughing.

Sally, giggling, said, "Remember the inflatable hunchback?"

"Remember when Clouseau is disguised as a sailor with a stuffed parrot hanging upside-down off his shoulder?"

"How about: 'I thought you said your dog didn't bite.' Remember the answer?"

"Sure. 'That's not my dog.'"

Now they were both doubled up in laughter.

When they stopped laughing, Sam said, "One of my goals in life is to rent all the *Pink Panther* movies and watch them straight through."

Then he added, rather wistfully, Sally thought, "But I never have time."

Sally nearly said, "That's your own fault," but she didn't.

The conversation got around to sports and television and books. Between bursts of laughter, Sally learned that Sam didn't know anything about sports or television because he was out of the country so much. "They don't telecast the Superbowl in Indonesia," he explained. So she was way ahead of him there. But, she estimated, he had read more books than anyone on earth—far more than she had, on both the fiction and non-fiction lists of the *New York Times*. "So would you if you spent most of your life on airplanes and in hotel rooms," he said. "But I'm up on movies—I see 'em in flight."

They were lolling in front of the fire, talking as if they'd known each other forever. Sally was very relaxed. She no longer cared about her burnt dinner. She was happy that Sam had dropped in. Nobody ever dropped in on her, she realized. She was also happy that Sam was obviously so much at home in her home, and seemed to like it as much as she did.

Never before had she realized how much fun it was just to sit and talk and do absolutely nothing.

Then Sam looked at his watch. "I have an early flight in the morning. I'd better go."

He stood up. "Thanks," he said. "I really enjoyed that." He picked up everything and whisked it to the kitchen.

"I did, too," Sally said, feeling strangely bereft, and then he was out the door and gone.

She leaned on the door and looked around the room. The pizza box and beer glasses were gone, and the only evidence that any of that had happened was the fire burning low in the fireplace. She shook her head and decided that Sam Thatcher was a figment of her imagination.

"The IRS auditor was in on Tuesday," Sally told Alicia. "So we got that year's taxes settled. Now we have two more years."

Alicia said, "I don't care about the taxes. I want to know what he was doing there, at your place."

Sally sighed. "I told you, I don't know. He just appeared, ate his pizza, talked a while and left. He's the strangest man I ever ran across. He's positively scary. Let's forget him. Let's order."

Sally and Alicia were at Shanghai Place, their favorite Chinese restaurant. True to their respective personalities, Sally was methodically going through the menu, item by item, trying each on in turn. Alicia always ordered the same things, her favorites.

After they had ordered, Alicia said, "Speaking of Sam Thatcher, I got the *Fortune* article. Very interesting. It hardly says anything personal, but it tells a lot about what he does." She reached into her tote bag and took out the magazine.

"Let me see that," said Sally.

"I thought you wanted to forget about Sam Thatcher," Alicia said, handing the magazine to Sally.

"Not completely," Sally said, skimming the article. "Thirty-six years old, economics B.A., Master's in Systems Analysis at U. of M. That doesn't tell us much."

Sally scanned the page and found what she was looking for. "The country risk expert is a recent phenomenon," Sally read aloud. "During the OPEC glory years, American banks were recycling billions of petrodollars into the Third World, without regard to politics or credit rating. Now the banks have learned through bitter experience that a country *can* go bankrupt, that debt can destabilize a government. They have come to rely on the risk analyst—the man who can tell them how risky that investment really is. A risk analyst takes into account everything from the health of the country's ruler to the value of the currency, and predicts how great the risk actually is. One of the most successful is Sam Thatcher, who, for example, predicted the fall of the Velasquez government in Venezuela almost to the day, and the Philippine default to the month."

"Impressive," said Alicia. "But how does he do it? It doesn't say in the article."

"Computers," said Sally. "And I'll bet he can't predict who will win the World Series or whether it will rain tomorrow. He's a human being just like the rest of us. Which means he's not perfect, either."

"Who said he was perfect?" Alicia said. "Who wants perfect?"

"Me," said Sally. "I'm waiting for the perfect man to come along, and when he does I'll recognize him right away. And he's not Sam Thatcher."

"Sally, what is the matter with you?" Alicia asked, plunging her chopsticks into her sweet and sour pork. "This man is obviously interested in you, and all you can do is back away."

Sally sighed. "It's not so obvious to me. But it's the same thing that's always been the matter, Alicia." She picked up a spring roll and swirled it in the soy sauce. "Anyone, male or female, who I can't trust scares me. You know me. You know that. And Sam Thatcher may be a hunk and rich and all that other wonderful stuff, but he's . . . volatile. He's exactly the wrong person for me. I can't even stand to work for him—it makes me crazy."

"What would you prefer?" Alicia asked. "The IRS?"

"At least," said Sally, "the IRS is utterly predictable. You know exactly what they want."

"Yeah," said Alicia. "Your life, your fortune and your sacred honor."

"I'm not really that stuffy, am I?" Sally said, picking up another potsticker between her chopsticks.

"Well, you're getting better. I'm sorry. I know it's hard for you, but you just seem to pass up some wonderful opportunities. Let go, have a fling. I'll be the first to applaud you."

"Okay, I'll have a fling. I'll sneak out of work tomorrow afternoon and go to a movie."

"That's not what I meant," Alicia said. "I meant, run away some place romantic with Sam Thatcher."

Sally started laughing. "Sam Thatcher is too busy running to run away. His idea of someplace romantic is probably Zambeziland."

"Where?" said Alicia.

A week later, Sam stuck his head around the doorjamb of the room where Sally and her two bookkeepers were working, this time on this year's taxes.

"Do you have a passport?" he asked.

Sally looked up. "Are you speaking to me?"

Sam nodded.

"No," Sally said. "Why?"

"Just wondering," said Sam, disappearing again, leaving a mystified Sally.

But she and her two employees were used to his strange ways, so she didn't think anything more about it until four days later when Sam came walking in after an overnight trip to San Francisco and found Sally talking to Marcy at the front desk.

"Come into my office a minute," he said to Sally.

Aha, she thought, following him. Now I can get him to sign that IRS 843 that's been sitting on his desk for a week. She looked at the desktop, where the form should have been, but it was obviously buried under several inches of other papers. It might be easier to photocopy another one, she was thinking, when Sam spoke.

"I want you to come to London with me. I need a tax expert."

"I beg your pardon?" Sally croaked. "Did you say something about me going to London? I've never been to

London in my life." The very thought was making her head spin. She decided she had misheard it.

"I need a tax expert to go with me. You have to get a passport."

Sally dropped into the leather chair in front of his desk and peered at him closely to see if he still looked sane. He was looking back at her with the faintest of grins.

"But . . ."

"But what?" he said.

"But I've never been out of the country before." Sally confessed.

"So now's your chance." he said reasonably.

"But people don't go to London first," she told him. "They go to Mexico or Canada."

"You can go there later," Sam said.

"And I don't know anything about foreign taxes. I only know U.S. taxes," she protested.

"I've got a copy of the Zambeziland tax code right here," Sam said.

"The Zambeziland tax code?" said Sally, having horrid flashbacks to what she had said to Alicia.

"Yes, a London bank consortium wants to invest in Zambeziland. They want my advice. I need to know about the tax structure."

"I'm not even sure where Zambeziland is," Sally spluttered.

"It doesn't matter, we're not going there. I was in Zambeziland a few weeks ago. Read the tax code and explain it to me."

"But I only read English," Sally said.

"The tax code is written in English," said Sam. "We leave in two days."

"I can't go, I don't have my shots."

"You don't need any," said Sam.

"I haven't got a passport."

"Go to the Passport Office in the Federal Building and you can get one in 24 hours. Expedited procedures," Sam told her.

"But I can't leave my job," Sally protested, and then realized that she was looking at her employer, who was now grinning broadly, if crookedly.

"We leave Wednesday morning. Be at the airport at nine. Your ticket will be at the airline counter with your name on it. The flight leaves at eleven. The weather is cold and rainy in March in London so bring your umbrella."

"But . . ." Sally said one last time. "But . . . I'm . . ."

"Here," said Sam, shuffling through the papers on his desk and pulling out a thick bound book. "This is the Zambeziland tax code. Read it tonight. I'll explain more on the plane."

He handed it to her. She stood up, feeling as if her legs were not functioning properly, and left his office. She staggered down the hall trying not to hold on to the wall, and then dropped into her chair and tried to tell herself that she had hallucinated it, but the weight of the tax code in her lap was enough to assure her that she hadn't.

Then she picked up the telephone and called Acme Temps. "Mary? This is Sally Forbes. Have you got another job available for a CPA? I can't take this one any longer."

There was a pause.

"Nothing. Not for two months? I can't go without work for two months."

After another pause, she said, "No, I won't take that much of a pay cut. I guess I'll just have to get along here. I'll tell you about it when I get back from London. Bye."

She put down the receiver. She looked in the phone book and dialed another number. "Hello? What do I need to bring down there to get a passport?"

* * *

After she'd received a phone call from a frantic Sally, Alicia had come to Sally's apartment.

"Calm down, Sally," she said. "I'd love to be going to London with that gorgeous creature."

"I know you would, Alicia," Sally said through clenched teeth as she tried to figure out how to get one more pair of shoes into her suitcase. "But I don't. I don't like to do things on the spur of the moment. It upsets me. I am a person who needs routine. I'm a CPA. CPAs don't go flying off to London."

"Where do CPAs fly off to?" Alicia said. "Did you remember to stop the newspaper?"

"CPAs don't fly off to anywhere. They stay home with their plants and their spreadsheets. And no, I didn't remember to stop the paper. You'll have to do that. I've got a list . . ."

"I'll take care of everything," said Alicia. "Just stop fussing. Enjoy yourself. You're going to be flying off to romantic London with the man who gets all the mash notes. Lucky you!"

"Romantic London! First of all, it's a business trip. He wants tax advice. And Sam Thatcher said it was cold and rainy, and I've heard stories—they have no central heating and Jack the Ripper and terrible plumbing. And as far as the man who gets a lot of mash notes—remember, they're all from strangers."

Alicia took Sally by the arm and said, "Listen to me, kiddo. I am your oldest and best friend. And I know you, and I know all about you. And you are protesting too much. You really like Sam Thatcher, I can tell. And you're missing the boat. He takes you out to eat, he drops in at your apartment, and now he's taking you to London. Why don't you try realizing you're lucky?"

Sally shook Alicia's hand off her arm and went back to her suitcase. "I am a stable person. I like to plan. I like to stay home. I like to cook a good dinner, and then sit in front of a cozy fire in the fireplace, and do some needlepoint and watch a nice funny TV show. I like to know exactly where I am going to be the day after tomorrow."

"So? What's wrong with that?"

"What's wrong with it is that Sam Thatcher is completely different from me. He's always flying off at a moment's notice, he doesn't seem to plan, and his life-style is exactly the opposite of mine. I want a man who is steady and safe and trustworthy. And I'll find him someday. But he isn't Sam Thatcher. Sam is a disaster waiting to happen."

"Now I know you really are interested in him," Alicia said. "Confess."

"All right, I *could* get very interested, but I'm not going to let that happen. I know what's good for me. And he's not. And I'm not good for him, either. I'm not even sure he's interested in me, either. I've devoted a lot of thought to this. I know what I'm doing."

"Your choice," said Alicia. "But at least enjoy your trip to London. Or your fling."

Sally made a rude noise, and tightened the strap on her suitcase. "You know this is only the third time in my life I have ever been on an airplane, don't you?"

"I love flying," said Alicia.

"I'm petrified of it," Sally said. "But there's no other way to get to London."

Chapter Three

At the airport, Sam recognized the symptoms—the sweaty hands, the pale face, the too perky replies—right away.

"Are you nervous about flying?" he asked, as they stood in line at the ticket counter.

"No, not at all," squeaked Sally.

"Have you flown a lot before?"

"A little," Sally said, kicking her suitcase ahead of her.

"Ever flown first class?"

"No."

"Here, let me help," said Sam, putting her suitcase on the scale beside the check-in counter. "Ever flown on a jumbo jet?"

"No. They look like they're too big to fly, to me," she said with a wan smile, fishing out her ticket for the clerk.

"Do you have your passport, Miss Forbes?"

There was a pause while Sally fished in her purse.

"I can't find it!" Sally's voice rose in sudden panic.

"Here," said Sam. "It's in your left hand."

"Oh." Sally took several deep breaths. The clerk ran some numbers on his computer terminal, dismantled Sally's ticket, and then put it back together in a different order and handed it to her.

"Have a nice trip, Miss Forbes," he said.

"Thank you," said Sally, and then to Sam she added, "Do you mind if I go sit down while you check in?"

"Go right ahead," Sam said.

When Sam produced his passport, even the jaded ticket clerk did a double-take at the extra pages of visas.

"Have a nice flight, Mr. Thatcher. Your flight is boarding now at Gate 23."

Good timing, thought Sam, walking through security behind Sally. That would give her less time to think about it. He'd noticed her legs—nice legs though they were—looked wobbly. She was being pretty classy about her fear, he decided. She wouldn't admit it for the world. He liked that. He could sympathize, but not understand, being afraid to fly. He was afraid of other things, but not airplanes. He felt bad about it—he knew he had shaken her to her shoes by insisting she go to London with him, but he couldn't think of any other way to do it. All he could do now was try his best to find a cure for her fright.

And, he thought, the double martinis he saw going down the gullets of his fellow passengers in the airport bar weren't the cure.

He took her arm in the jetway, saying, "Let me guess. Your last flight was in a much smaller plane, and you were crowded in with with a million people, and there was a line a mile long for the restroom, and you bounced all over the sky."

"How did you know?" Sally sounded surprised.

"I fly that way, too," he said, "Sometimes worse. When I have to. Wait'll you fly on this one. You'll never be nervous again."

They were, as he suspected, almost the only passengers in first-class, and the flight attendant greeted them by name and hovered while they settled in the wide seats. Sally was visibly relaxing.

"See that spiral staircase back there?" Sam said. "That goes up to the lounge, which is usually empty. You can go up and do exercises when you need to stretch your legs."

The safety instructions made her nervous again. Sam noticed she even checked to see that there was a flotation device under her seat and looked at the diagram for the nearest emergency exit. It occurred to him that he had never done that in his life, and that it wasn't a bad idea.

He tried talking to her during takeoff, but she didn't seem to hear a word he said. She just gripped his forearm so hard that he feared he would never be able to use that hand again.

Finally he said, "You can open your eyes now. We're off the ground for good."

She blinked and looked around. They were climbing through clouds and not bumping in the slightest.

"It feels like we're on the Expressway, this is so smooth," she said in obvious surprise. The pressure on his forearm let up. And then clamped down again. "How does the pilot know there isn't another plane out there in those clouds?"

"Radar," said Sam, and then they broke through the clouds into brilliant sunshine in an empty sky.

"It's beautiful!" exclaimed Sally, letting go of Sam in order to put her nose to the window. "It's just like flying! I can see the shadow of the plane on the clouds, and there's a rainbow around it!"

Sam rubbed his arm and flexed his fingers and wondered if he would have a bruise.

As she looked out, transfixed, he watched her and wondered, why am I so attracted to her?

He thought of the first time he'd seen her, really seen her. It was like a snapshot. In it he could see everything about her: that gray suit, the purple sweater, the fact that she had three manila folders in her hand. She was standing in front of his desk, with a little of the hunter's pride—she finally tracked him down in his lair. She'd treated him as her equal, and he liked that. The shining jet black hair hung in two soft arcs to her shoulders, setting off the fair complexion, those high cheekbones, and those incredible eyes, fringed by dark lashes. She'd seemed very self-contained so that it took a few moments to realize how very pretty she was.

So he'd taken her with him for a drink after work, using his best don't-give-'em-a-chance-to-say-no technique, and was both pleased and disappointed that she seemed genuinely interested in his taxes and not in him. Looking over at her now and seeing that she had pulled out the Zambeziland tax code, Sam smiled wryly to himself. After that damned magazine article, when all those woman began ambushing him, it was a relief to find one who was interested in his taxes. But it was a disappointment that taxes seemed all she was interested in—or was it a challenge? Sam wondered.

But there was more to Sally's attraction than that. This life—half of it spent on airplanes, rocketing back and forth across the International Dateline, living in hotels—could be made very, very comfortable. But it was beginning to get a little old. Or maybe he, Sam, was getting old. He was starting to think about something a little more stable, normal. Not quite the house in the suburbs with crabgrass, but something more like that than a single hotel room.

So, taking all these things into consideration, he had decided to do something about Sally. It was not easy. He quickly learned that she was organized down to her toes, which, perhaps perversely, he found attractive. He checked out her apartment and learned she was as domesticated as a tabby cat. That, too, made it better. She led a stable life, all right. And that appealed to him. He also began to sense a vulnerability about her, one that brought out his protective instincts. Like her fear of flying. He looked over at her again. She had a happy smile on her face. One fear down, he thought, with a few more to go.

So having concluded that she had a lot of the things he was looking for, he thought about taking her to England. He was aware that he was attacking the problem of Sally in the same way that he attacked any problem—gather data, figure the risks, and then decide. He knew the risk was very great—at the ninety percent level—that she'd get permanently mad at him when he pulled The Surprise on her. But, thought Sam, nothing ventured, nothing gained.

Just then the pilot came on the intercom. "Welcome to Flight 10, Ladies and Gentlemen. This is your Captain speaking. We have reached our cruising altitude of 40,000 feet. Our speed is 500 knots. Our gross weight at takeoff was 700,000 pounds. We will be taking the polar route, and there will be cloud cover most of the way. The weather in London is rainy, and the temperature will be in the low 40s. We hope you enjoy the flight."

Sam glanced over at Sally, who was looking shocked.

"What's the matter?" he asked.

"Seven hundred thousand pounds? And we got off the ground?"

"Forty thousand feet off," Sam said.

"Wow," said Sally. "You know, I really like this flying business."

First came the food, on china and crystal, with real silver, and then came the first movie, and if Sally so much as wriggled her nose, a flight attendant was there inquiring as to her wants.

It was, Sally realized, pure luxury. First class was first class. She took off her shoes, wriggled her toes and slumped in the seat, and when she felt the need, she got up and wandered around the plane and looked in the back and felt sorry for the people crammed in there.

Sam had dozed through most of the movie and was reading a paperback when she got back from one of her wanderings. She felt guilty and dug out the Zambeziland Tax Code again. This was a business trip, she reminded herself.

"If you look down, you can see Greenland," said a flight attendant passing by.

Sally pressed her nose to the scratched window and looked down. Sure enough, between the patches of cloud, she could see what appeared to be a frozen ocean, with a few streaks of brown earth. Then the plane banked into a turn and all she could see was cloudless blue atmosphere.

"Whee!" Sally exclaimed. Then she looked back down at the tax code.

"That's pretty dull stuff," said Sam. "I appreciate what you're doing."

"Actually, it isn't that dull," Sally said. "I find it interesting, comparing it with our tax code. Why don't you tell me why you want to know this? What does going to London have to do with taxes in Zambeziland?"

Sam stretched luxuriously, yawned, and said, "Maybe nothing, maybe everything."

"That's ambiguous," Sally said.

"I know, but that's the best I can do at the moment," Sam said. "It all depends."

"On what?" Sally asked. "I don't even understand what you do, much less what I'm doing here."

"Well, in this particular case a group of banks has been asked to loan several million pounds sterling to the country of Zambeziland for investment in heavy equipment for diamond mining. It's risky for two reasons: South Africa, Zambeziland's neighbor, has a stranglehold on the diamond market, and Zambeziland itself is a fledgling undeveloped country. These banks have all been burned before on similar deals, not necessarily in Zambeziland, but all over the Third World. They've made billions in bad loans—otherwise known as the international debt crisis. Heads of state have run off with the money, or it's been lost through corruption, or the bottom dropped out of oil prices, and now banks and even governments are toppling. Now they've learned their lesson. So they ask people like me what I think."

"So how do you know what you think?" Sally asked.

"I get the data, the statistics, and I talk to people, and I nose around."

"And then you run it through a computer?" Sally asked.

"And then I run it through a computer, but that's not all. A lot of it is gut feeling."

"Gut feeling?" Sally said, aghast. "How about bottom line? Does that count?"

"Sure bottom line counts, but gut feeling counts more," Sam said.

Then the second movie came to life and sound on the screen. Sam watched, while Sally thought about what he had just said. She couldn't believe her ears. He couldn't have meant what he said about analyzing things by gut feeling. That was about on a par with looking in a crystal ball, or reading tea leaves. Sam Thatcher was paid thousands of dollars by the likes of the Bank of the Far East or Brown and Morrison for an analysis of his *gut feelings*? Sally shook her head. No, that couldn't be.

She leaned her seat back as far as it would go and concentrated on the movie. The first one had been outstanding, she thought, but this, though a critical success, was, well, boring. The next thing she knew she was being gently shaken by the shoulder, and Sam was saying, "We're coming in to Heathrow."

She sat up groggily.

"You've been asleep three hours," said Sam grinning his crooked grin.

"I wasn't sleeping, just resting my eyes, actually," she said as the flight attendant came by to check the seatbelts and make sure her seat was upright.

Sally was determined not to be nervous on the landing. But the control tower didn't cooperate. They were stacked up circling Heathrow for half an hour, bumping through clouds so thick that Sally couldn't see the end of the wing. It all began to come back to her. She began to imagine a hundred other jets out there in the murk only a wing tip away. She imagined wind shear, she imagined metal fatigue, she imagined the air controller in the tower making a mistake. She knew the statistics, the dangers, the possibilities, and they all ran through her head in ascending order of horribleness. She glanced over at Sam, who was reading a copy of *The Economist*, which the flight attendant had handed him, appearing perfectly calm.

Without even looking at her, he put out a hand and covered hers—the one that was gripping the armrest so tightly that her knuckles were white.

"Relax," he said. "Statistically, you're safer up here than on the Expressway. And my gut feeling says that we'll be down in a few minutes, safe and sound."

And even though Sally didn't believe in gut feeling, there was something so warm and reassuring about his hand on hers that she didn't even notice the bump that meant they were on the ground. In fact, she didn't notice they were down until the jets went into reverse, throwing her forward against the seatbelt.

Heathrow was a nightmare, as Sam had warned her earlier, and all the first-class treatment in the world didn't help in getting yourself or your baggage through the interminable lines at Immigration. Sally was thrown for a loop immediately, when the immigration agent smiled broadly and said something she could not understand. She asked him to repeat it, and when she still did not understand, she said "Yes." Then she said, "No," to a second question, and the man smiled again, stamped her passport and waved her on.

"They don't speak *English* here," she said to Sam as they headed into London in the back seat of a tall black taxi with a driver who persisted in driving on the wrong side of the road.

The hotel was a pile of red stone covered with nightmare Victoriana, very plush, very expensive, and very comfortable. Sally's room overlooked a parklike square, full of bare trees and bushes, with walks and benches here and there, and with a high, spiked wrought iron fence around it. Sam had told her that this was not a public park—you had to have a key to get in. Sally thought that was terribly undemocratic, but it appealed to her CPA instincts—the park was the cleanest, neatest place she had ever seen. She looked down at the traffic flowing around it and decided that most vehicles in London seemed to be on the verge of tipping over—double decker buses and high narrow black taxis.

Then, slightly dizzy and totally confused as to what time it was, she unpacked everything, hanging clothes in the closet, and refolding her underwear and putting it into drawers.

Not knowing what else to do, she took a long hot shower, washed her hair, brushed and flossed her teeth, and got into her red flannel nightshirt. She washed out the bra and panties she had worn and hung them on the heated towel bar to dry. Then she wondered, what next? Sam had disappeared just after they'd checked in, leaving her with no instructions, so she assumed she was on her own. She couldn't think of anything to do, so she crawled into bed, taking the Zambeziland tax code with her. Her watch said nine o'clock, but she knew that wasn't right. She had just reached foreign investment credits, which she thought might be important, when she drifted off to sleep.

Sally awoke to the insistent knocking at her door, and sat straight up in bed, confused. Finally she remembered she was in London, in a hotel, and realized the knocking was getting louder and louder. A fire! she thought, jumping out of bed and racing to the door. She flung it open.

Outside stood Sam Thatcher. "Are you all right?" he said with real concern in his voice. "I've been calling your room number for the last half hour."

"I'm fine," Sally said, groggily. "I guess I was so sound asleep I didn't hear it."

"What are you doing asleep at this hour?" Sam asked.

"What are you doing awake at this hour?" Sally managed, trying to get the cobwebs out of her head.

"Do you know what time it is?"

"Bedtime," mumbled Sally. "Whatever time it is, it's bedtime."

"Local time is six-thirty p.m.," Sam told her. "If you go to bed now you'll wake up at two in the morning and be off schedule for the rest of the time you are in London. I made dinner reservations for seven in the dining room."

Suddenly Sally's brain kicked in and she realized two things. Sam was somehow inside her room and the door was closed, and she was somehow dressed in her ancient flannel nightshirt, and her hair was still damp. She was appalled. And worse, threatened. She was not so puritanical that the idea of a man in her hotel room while she was dressed in a nightshirt—it was more than modest—was any big deal. No, it was not that. It was *this* man in her hotel room that made her nervous. He was so unpredictable, she told herself. But even worse, he was so—sexy. It had never occurred to her before, but now, in this situation there were these—vibrations, waves of something emanating from him in her direction. Suddenly he seemed very, very large, and . . . the word dangerous leaped into her mind.

Even as all these . . . emotions, gut feelings overcame her, Sally gave herself a rapid mental scolding "Don't be silly," she said to herself. "It doesn't compute. He's not dangerous, he's just disorganized."

And to Sam, she said, "I'd really rather just stay here. I'm not hungry."

"I really recommend doing it my way," said Sam, with the ghost of a grin. Sally did not like the way he was eyeing the nightshirt. Maybe he *was* dangerous.

"Doing what your way?" she said, heading for the closet for her bathrobe.

"Eating a good dinner at the correct time and then staying up until ten or eleven o'clock," he said as if he were talking to a five-year-old. "Believe me, I know all about jet lag, and that's the only way to beat it."

Sally struggled into her pink chenille bathrobe, and felt a little less vulnerable. He could eye the front of the bathrobe all day long—the only thing of interest there was a white chenille bird of some sort.

"Is that your gut feeling?" she asked.

"No, school of hard knocks," he told her. "I have credit for something like half a million frequent flyer miles on my cards. If I ever used them all, I'd bust the airlines. So I ought to know. Come on. Get dressed. I'll meet you downstairs in fifteen minutes." He turned toward the door.

That was so nonthreatening that Sally decided she had misread the whole situation. She began to think he was right. She would change clothes, go to dinner and then... She touched her hair and realized it was still very damp. "I can't go. My hair. I forgot my hair dryer. I ..."

"Your hair's just fine," Sam said, reaching out and touching it just above her ear.

Sally expected him to draw back his hand, but he did not. She was frozen, feeling that light touch on her hair, as if the contact had changed some imperceptible but life-giving equilibrium within. He, too, seemed shaken, unable to move.

She raised her eyes and saw his warm brown ones searching her face. She tried to lift a hand, either to touch him, or ward him off, she did not know which, and then somehow she was in his arms, and his mouth was coming down on hers, and there was a roaring in her ears that was very like the muted roar of a jet engine. As if she'd done it a thousand times, she reached up and put her arms around his neck. She felt his long lean body next to hers and closed her eyes and marveled at how perfect it all felt, how warm and wonderful and natural this was. And then his mouth met hers, softly and tenderly, and all thought left her.

His hands moved down her back until they reached just the right places, hers moved upward to bury themselves in his thick brown hair. Now his mouth was hungry, seeking, exploring and then overwhelming. The slow, sweet icy fire began somewhere in the core of her and spread outward along some secret network heretofore unknown to every cell and nerve ending in her body. And when the kiss had gone on for half an eternity, and Sally's knees began to buckle, she knew that the next thing he would do would be to pick her up and carry her toward that big satin-covered bed and . . .

All at once she felt her wet hair on her face, realized that she was wearing a faded chenille bathrobe, and that she was standing in the middle of a hotel room in a totally strange country, seven or eight time zones from home. And that she was being kissed by—and kissing back—a man she hardly knew, an erratic genius who lived out of a suitcase and advised people to make multimillion dollar loans to countries called Zambeziland on the basis of his gut feeling. None of it computed. It was all wrong. She was a CPA.

"Mmmmmmm!" she said, pulling away and crossing her arms protectively on her chest as she backed off.

Sam did not try to follow. He just stood there, grinning that crooked grin. Sally had to admit it was a wonderful, sexy grin, but the rest of it was just too much for her. She was in full retreat.

Sam said, "I've been wanting to do that ever since I first saw you."

"You have?" Sally squeaked. "Why?"

"If you need to ask, I'm not telling," said Sam, grinning and going out the door.

Dinner was wonderful, and very, very expensive, but Sally knew it was a tax write-off. She let him do the ordering—something called pheasant soufflé, followed by Northumberland pork in a cream sauce. Plus a good French white wine. He obviously knew what he was doing, but then she remembered his frequent flyer miles and his hotel room home and realized he must eat out three meals a day. How dreadful, she thought, almost feeling sorry for him.

"I'm amazed," she said, afterward. "I heard British food was awful."

"A lot of it is," he told her, "just like any country. But I think the perfidious French probably spread disinformation about British cooking. In revenge for Waterloo."

Sam was looking very contented and unjet-lagged across the crisp linen tablecloth. Sally had deliberately put that strange kiss and the confusion it had caused out of her mind—CPAs could do that kind of thing. It was like using a computer program. Hit the Save button and go on to the next spreadsheet. File it under "Anomalies." You could always pull it up out of your random access memory when needed. Now it was not needed. Now she felt she was beginning to get control of the situation, for the first time during the trip. And she realized that the best defense was a good offense. Now, Sally decided, was the time to ask questions—while Sam was full of good food and good wine. She wanted some explanations and she was in question mode.

"Why do you live the way you live?" she asked.

Sam seemed startled. "What do you mean?"

"I mean, you live out of a suitcase. In a hotel room. Don't you get tired of it?"

That seemed to take him off-guard. "I had an apartment once, but I traveled so much that it just didn't make sense."

"Don't you miss home cooking?"

"Well, I don't miss my own cooking, if that's what you mean."

"Did you have a mother and father and a family and all that? Or were you born in a hotel room, too?"

Sam laughed. "You think I grew up in the Plaza like Eloise?"

"Did you?"

"No. I grew up in a real house, with real parents and a real brother and a real dog in a real city. In a suburb of Chicago, as a matter of fact. You've heard of it?" Sam grinned that crooked heartbreaking grin.

"Of course, I've heard of Chicago. It's in the state of Cleveland, I think," said Sally, deadpan. "What did you do when you were growing up in a real house, with real parents, and a real dog?"

"And a real brother, don't forget. Let's see. I had a paper route and I mowed lawns and I shoveled snow and I was an Eagle Scout and on the high school basketball team and I fought with my brother a lot."

"Who won?"

"He did, until I got bigger than he was."

"And where are your real parents and your real brother and your real dog now?"

"My parents are still in the same house in the same suburb, my brother's a surgeon in Milwaukee and has three kids, and the dog...well, you don't want to hear what happened to Henry the Dog. It was terrible."

"So, coming from a stable background like that," Sally began thoughtfully, "how can you stand—"

"How can I stand the way I live? Well, I've been doing this for quite awhile, and there are times, I'll admit, that I get tired of it. But for now, this kind of living is pretty comfortable. Don't you agree?"

Sally had to agree.

"And I seem to thrive on the jet lag and I enjoy what I do. I feel I'm making a contribution. I'm good at it. And, so far, I never get tired of going places and seeing things and talking to people. Eventually, I'll settle down in some suburb and start moving lawns again. Not quite yet, though. I plan to give it a few more weeks, anyway."

Then Sam looked across the table at Sally very solemnly and said, "I can see you totting all that up in your mind. Debits and credits, accounts receivable and payable. Now it's my turn. You, my purple-eyed Indian friend, are the most compulsive person I ever met. Now that is a real plus for a CPA, but it must put a real crimp in your life-style. Have you ever done anything impulsive in your life?"

Sally was offended but she remembered that he had answered her equally impertinent questions. Tit for tat. She took a last sip of her dry crisp white wine, and said, "I can't think of anything on the spur of the moment, but I'm sure I have."

Then she didn't understand why Sam laughed.

Sam said, "Tell me about your real parents and real house and real brother. It's only fair, after I bared all."

There was a long long silence.

Sally gritted her teeth. It was less painful to tell the truth than to lie about it—she knew from past experience.

"Mine isn't as nice and all-American as yours," she began. "My father was an alcoholic, though he made a good enough living, and my sister and I grew up with all the problems that children of alcoholics have. We learn not to trust anyone, because our alcoholic parents are so undependable. My sister became a librarian in order to cope with it, and I became a CPA. Those are both professions where it helps to be compulsive."

"I see," said Sam, very kindly. "I'm sorry to hear it. You must have had a very hard time of it."

"Not all that bad," Sally began amending. "My mother was terrific and handled it all very well. And my father's okay now. More than okay. He's a commercial artist, and a lot of it was his work environment. So they bought a ranch in Idaho. My mom loves running it, since she grew up on a ranch, and my father's able to work there better, without distractions. My sister and I go there every Christmas, at least. It's really beautiful there.''

Sam looked at her across the table with an expression she was unable to read.

"Does it bother you to talk about it?" he asked softly.

''No, not really,'' said Sally. But it did. It seemed to her that he was five feet closer than he had been before. She began getting a trapped feeling, the same trapped feeling she had gotten since childhood. It happened whenever anyone got too close to the things she'd so carefully buried. Sometimes she even had trouble breathing when people got this close to her. So she added, ''I just wish I hadn't started this conversation at all.''

Sam said, ''I think it's a fine conversation.''

"It's not the kind of conversation that should go on between employer and employee," Sally said. There, that should put some distance between them, she thought.

"That's true," said Sam, "but we aren't employer and employee now. Now I'm just taking you out to dinner. But I'll change the subject for you. I'll explain why I kissed you."

Sally suddenly felt her face turn red. Now she could barely breathe at all.

"I kissed you for a lot of reasons: because you're terrific-looking, because I felt like it, because of a lot of things, but also because I wanted to see if there was anything impulsive about you—if you could do anything spur of the moment. If you could take a risk. And, it proved something. You can. Very well indeed. You should let yourself go more often."

Sally was appalled. "I ..." she said. "I think ..."

"You have to learn to trust yourself first," Sam said, "before you can trust anyone else." He paused a moment, and then said, "Boy, was that profound."

Sally said, "I . . ."

"Here's another one. Kissing is like flying—once you've done it first class, you never want to stop, right?"

Sally looked up, saw that Sam was grinning from ear to ear. She thought for a moment and burst out laughing.

"That was awesome," she said.

Suddenly, she felt much better.

After that, they each drank two cups of coffee, and when Sam had paid the check, they bundled into their coats and walked around the square a couple of times. It was cold and windy, but not raining. Finally, it was ten o'clock and even Sam agreed it was late enough to go to sleep.

He escorted her to her room—his was on a different floor—and politely shook her hand at the door.

Sally, suddenly exhausted, barely got out of her clothes and fell into the bed. She did not remove her makeup or floss her teeth. She slept soundly for two hours, and woke up again. She tried a hot shower, climbed back into bed and lay, tossing and turning, trying to figure out Sam Thatcher. She couldn't get it together. It didn't compute. And she was a Certified Public Accountant.

Chapter Four

Toward morning, Sally fell asleep again, and woke when her telephone rang.

"Good morning," came Sam's deep voice over the phone.

"Mmmf," said Sally, finally getting the receiver to her ear by turning over on her back and coming up out of the covers a bit.

"It's nine o'clock, and you have the day off," Sam said. "I'll be back about five. There's plenty to do, so enjoy yourself. The British Museum is just a couple of blocks away."

"Pardon?" said Sally, waking slightly, more from the cold air going down her neck than from anything else.

Sam repeated what he had said, and added, "Be ready at five—dressed. In the lobby."

"Wait," said Sally, finally beginning to wake up. "Why do I have the day off? Where are you going? Why do I have to be dressed at five? What for?"

But Sam was gone.

So Sally, deciding that this would be the only time in her entire life that she could tour London, leaped out of bed, got dressed, had a quick breakfast, and with the help of the hotel concierge managed to be the last passenger aboard the Grand London Tour Number 8 bus. She had chosen Number 8 because it offered the most famous sights and sites in the least time. It was cost effective.

She carried the Zambeziland tax code with her and took an occasional glance at it in spare moments, to overcome the feeling of guilt at not working. She figured that the five o'clock deadline given by Sam meant that her tax knowledge would be drawn upon then. She felt prepared, but taking small peeks into the book while waiting in line at the Tower of London, for instance, soothed her conscience.

She barely made it back in enough time to shower and change clothes. Sam was waiting in the lobby.

"You look very nice," he said approvingly as she approached. Then before she could say anything, he took her arm and escorted her to a taxi. After a few blocks the taxi pulled up in front of a half-timbered building, which turned out to be a tavern once frequented by Samuel Johnson. In a wood-paneled room, Sam ordered roast beef and Yorkshire pudding and some other strange English things—trifle, for instance—and then leaned back in his chair.

"There. Now we have nearly two hours to enjoy this."

Something about the way he said that gave Sally an ominous feeling. "What happens in two hours?" she asked, feeling a little like Anne Boleyn at the Tower of London.

"Theater," said Sam. "I hope that's okay with you."

"Theater?" Sally said, astounded, her voice rising. "I thought this was a business trip. I thought I'd be asked about the Zambeziland tax code. I thought . . ."

"Don't you want to go to the theater? I had to pull every string I had to get two tickets on such short notice," Sam said with a look and tone that Sally took to be false wounded innocence. She knew he was playing games with her. She just didn't know which game it was.

"Of course I want to go," Sally said, beginning to feel like a dog in the manger. "It's just that I'd like to know when I get to talk about the Zambeziland tax code."

"All in good time," said Sam. "It hasn't come up yet."

The following day, which Sally also had "off," she took Tour #9, which included a very chilly boat trip. That night Sam had managed tickets to the opera. The day after that, Sunday, Sam took her with him to the country place of the president of a chartered bank, and thereafter they roamed the back roads in the English countryside. A weak sun shone down for the first time since they'd set foot at Heathrow. Sam had rented a car, and Sally marveled at the way he was able to drive on the left side of the road without flinching. She was constantly stepping out in front of cars because she looked the wrong way at the intersection. The word Zambeziland was never mentioned that day.

On Monday morning Sam had asked Sally for a short—not more than one page—description of investment tax credits in the Zambeziland tax code. He looked at her work, said, "Hmm" and put it down. "Can you amuse yourself until about noon?" he asked.

"Sure, I'll go to the British Museum," she said. "What happens at noon?"

"We'll be through here," Sam told her.

"Through? That's all you wanted from me?"

"Talk to you about it when I get back," said Sam.

Sally walked the three blocks to the British Museum hunched in her lined raincoat, trying to hold an umbrella against the driving icy rain. She struggled through the door into the cavernous interior of the museum, checked her umbrella and kept her coat. She followed a map of the place on which she had methodically worked out a route that would touch on the most important things. There were thirty-four very important things, and twenty-seven important things, and thousands of interesting but not so famous things. She estimated she could spend one minute looking at each of the very importants, and thirty seconds walking in between. By the time she got to the Egyptian section, she was twelve minutes behind schedule. Further on was the room containing the Elgin Marbles, which Sally remembered the British had removed from the Acropolis in Athens. The Elgin Marbles were the most famous exhibit in the museum. She decided to skip the Egyptians to catch up on her schedule.

The Elgin Marbles were displayed around all four walls of a very large, temperature-controled double-doored room. In the center were backless wooden benches, and Sally immediately noticed, near one of them a docent was lecturing to a group of very serious-looking university students. She quietly went over and sat down, planning to get in on the lecture. In any case, she had a full five minutes here.

"...taken from the Parthenon," said the guide, "by Lord Thomas Elgin..."

Whew, thought Sally. It felt good to sit. Her back was starting to ache from walking on these marble floors.

"...overall design by Phidias, and the pedimental figures display the classical qualities..."

Gosh, thought Sally. These sculptures are really badly broken, some of them. She checked her watch. She had three more minutes. She stretched her legs out, wriggled her shoulders to ease the strain.

"...caryatid from the porch of the Erechtheum..."

A caryatid, Sally learned, was a statue of a woman that served as a pillar. This caryatid had held up the roof of a temple. At least, Sally thought wryly, the caryatid was using her head, which she, Sally, could not say for herself.

She had to admit that she should have enjoyed nearly every minute of the time she had been in London. She'd seen a lot in a short time, she was staying in a luxury hotel, eating the best food London had to offer. People would kill for a vacation like that, she knew. So why was she so... unhappy? No, not unhappy. More like uncomfortable.

"...Propylaea designed by Mnesicles is colonnade construction..."

And all the bits and bytes about Sam she had buried by hitting the Save button pushed themselves up onto her mental computer screen. Sam, thought Sally. Sam. The big question was: Why had he brought her here? It was now obvious that the tax structure of Zambeziland was window dressing. She'd wondered about it from the beginning, and then when he'd kissed her in the hotel room she'd started thinking he had some really nefarious purpose. Such as whisking her off to an ornate Victorian hotel, in foggy London town, against her will. What did they call that? White Slavery?

Without realizing it, she giggled out loud.

The lecturer paused and looked at her inquiringly.

Sally covered her mouth, and looked away.

"On the north wall are three statues representing..." continued the lecturer.

No, Sally thought to herself, it was obvious that White Slavery wasn't exactly what Sam had in mind. Because that one kiss had been the end of it. Which was odd. Surely he'd felt the same thing she had during that kiss, the way they seemed to fit together, the smooth, perfect way they'd seemed to know each other's...geography? It was also odd because Sam seemed to like her, to enjoy her. He certainly enjoyed surprising her. And she was beginning to like it herself. Beginning to expect it. Beginning to like the unexpected. She'd even liked flying.

"...fifth century B.C., the severe Doric of the Parthenon was offset by..."

Sally mused on. So how did she feel about Sam? She felt something. In fact, the more time she spent with him the more something she felt. She remembered all those letters from women—the letters signed with a lipstick kiss—and wondered if that was what she felt. She hoped not. Sure, there was sexual attraction, who wouldn't feel that about Sam? But there was more than that. It was a quickened heartbeat when he said, "Sally," for instance. It was a tenderness at times in the midsection, just below the ribs. Sally knew what that was.

The docent and the students all moved slowly away into the next room. Sally didn't even notice. She was staring at the caryatid, who seemed to be staring back.

So why was she suppressing all that she thought and felt about Sam? Sally knew why. It was Sam himself. His lifestyle was horrendous, in fact shocking, his energy ten times normal, his mind worked so quickly that he sometimes left her far behind, something that rarely happened to Sally. Just when she thought she could predict what he would say or do, he metamorphosed into a different Sam.

Another docent led another group of students, younger ones, this time, toward the bench were Sally sat. "These marbles were removed from the Acropolis in Athens by Lord Thomas Elgin," he said. "They were bought..."

To Sally, the CPA, with her need for neat columns and double entries, Sam was both fascinating and horrifying. He operated on gut feeling, she on the Internal Revenue Act of

1986, as amended. Sally had begun to realize that what he meant by gut feeling—intuition—was really just putting facts together in a different way, or using data that nobody else used. A sort of creativity, she supposed. And that was really out of her realm. The IRS, for instance, regarded "creative accounting" as a felony. Sam got paid for being creative: Sally would go to jail for it.

In short, Sally mused, staring blankly back at a noseless statue, she and Sam lived in entirely different worlds. She didn't understand him. She didn't know what he had in mind. She didn't trust him.

"...caryatid from the porch of the Erechtheum..." said the docent.

Sally sighed deeply.

The lecturer stopped and glared at her and cleared his throat. "As I was saying, the Propylaea, designed by Mnesicles, is colonnade construction..." he continued.

Furthermore, Sally thought, people like Sam didn't get involved with domesticated CPAs. She should never have told him about her alcoholic father. Now he pitied her. Or maybe he was just being polite. Damn. It didn't compute. She didn't know what she was doing here and she didn't understand Sam Thatcher at all. She was back to Go. She heaved another very large sigh.

The lecturer stopped, and all the students looked at her.

"Madam," said the lecturer in his museum voice, "might we ask you to sigh in the Assyrian room where it is less distracting? Thank you."

Sally blinked, looked at her watch and jumped up.

"I'm very sorry," she said, hurrying out the door. All that rumination had left her only an hour to see the rest of the British Museum. Even though she took a couple of minutes to redo her route, she was eighteen major exhibits short at the end of her tour. She ran back to the hotel, five minutes late, her only comfort being that it had stopped raining.

"You'll like the north," said Sam, as the rented Jaguar cleared the London suburbs and began picking up speed on M-1. The superhighway's big green signs gave Sally little chills. They read: To Scotland and the north.

"Why?" Sally asked. "What's there?"

"It's full of medieval towns with ancient cathedrals and castles," said Sam. "You can practically see characters out of Shakespeare acting out history there, they say."

"Why are you going there?" Sally persisted.

"I want to see it. I've never been there."

"And where are you going after that?" Sally very carefully did not use the word *we*.

"Probably Scotland."

"You don't know exactly where you're going?" Sally asked.

"Not exactly," Sam said, looking over at her in the passenger seat. "Does that bother you?"

"Of course it...doesn't." Sally sat up very straight against the shoulder seat belt. The tape deck was pouring out soft piano music, filling the plush interior of the car with modernist unresolved chords that seemed to Sally as aimless as Sam himself. The music topped it off. It was the icing on the cake. Sally started to read Sam the riot act.

"Yes, it does. It bothers me because it's just like the rest of this so-called business trip. You brought me along under false pretenses, you didn't need anything from me that some chartered accountant here couldn't do in five minutes. You never told me from one day to the next what you were doing, or what I was supposed to be doing."

Sally paused long enough to glare at Sam. His only reaction to this was a crooked grin that irritated her even more. She plunged on.

"Furthermore, now I don't know why I am going to the north. Do you have reservations? What if the car breaks down? How can you travel like this? How can you stand not to know where you are going?" She stopped again, realizing how she sounded.

Sam, still smiling, only said, "Which question do you want me to answer first?"

Sally said haughtily, "None of them. They're all rhetorical. I apologize for the tone of voice, but not the content." She quickly closed her mouth before any more came out. She couldn't believe she'd actually said all that. She wasn't sure she did want to know the answers—they might only reinforce what she suspected, which was the worst. She comforted herself with the fact that her outburst made her feel better, and it hadn't fazed Sam, much. Now he was whistling off-key along with the ghastly music.

She leaned back against the leather seat and crossed her arms and looked hard out the window. England consisted of rolling green hills, fields delineated by stone walls, a few trees and zillions of sheep, she decided. And cold rain. And blustery wind. And the English! They drove on the wrong side of the road and ate things with funny names, like bubble and squeak and spotted dick, and weighed themselves in stones instead of pounds. And they didn't talk like they did on Masterpiece Theater, so she couldn't understand them. They were really disorganized, the English.

Then on the horizon, on a hill, she saw chimneys and made out a mansion through the leafless trees. It was vast and red brick and Georgian—she could make out fanlights—and there was a tree-lined lane winding across miles of fields to its door. Sally remembered Westminster Abbey and St. Paul's and The Tower and decided that though this architectural evidence of a long and great history might prove the British a great people, they'd done it despite the disorganization. Wasn't that the British way? Muddle through? Hmmph, she thought.

Just then Sam said, "Let me ask you a question, if I may."

Sally shot a glance over at him to see the expression on his face. She couldn't. He was watching the road, looking craggy and handsome and relaxed, in jeans and a sweater and boot shoes. He looked just like an American tourist, she thought. "Okay, ask," she said.

"If I'd said I was going to London on business for a few days and then spending a week on vacation in the north of England and invited you to go along with me, what would you have said?"

"If you had invited me along on a vacation? What would I have said?" Sally echoed, not grasping what he was saying. "What do you think I would have said? I hardly know you. I'd have said no, of course."

"Well, now you see why I told you it was work," said Sam.

"But I still don't understand."

"You will, shortly," Sam said. "Look, there's the turn-off to Durham. Let's see what's there."

Durham was wonderful, an ancient city made of stone with a cathedral in which were buried saints with names like Cuthbert.

Despite all Sally's misgivings, they found a cozy, delightful bed-and-breakfast place, in a house built in the twelfth century with two-foot thick walls made with stones from the Roman Wall further north. The plumbing was peculiar, but the rooms were terrific, done up in bright chintz and antiques. Tossing their bags into their rooms, Sam and Sally trudged through the streets, some of them cobblestone. While the light lasted, Sam took pictures as assiduously as any other tourist.

The light faded, and the rain, rolling in over the soft worn green hills, arrived at about the same time, and Sam and Sally ducked into the nearest doorway. This turned out to be an inn, famous for its food, and there just happened to be a table for two, right by the big stone fireplace. Sally wondered if this happened to everybody, or if you had to be Sam Thatcher not to get caught in the middle of an empty field by the rain and the dark, or never have to wait for a table.

When they were seated and comfortable and had started on the pâté, Sally said, "I have been thinking over what you said in the car, and I believe that you said that you brought me to England against my will and under false pretenses, in order to go on vacation with you. Isn't that kidnapping, or something?"

Sam looked thoughtful. He swallowed his wine. He spread some more pâté on some melba toast, very, very carefully, as if it were to be on display in an art gallery, and then put it down.

Finally, looking straight at her, he said, "I guess you could say that."

"Oh," Sally said. "Well, I guess it's okay, since it's already been done, but I would like an explanation. I got over being mad in the car. Did you leave a ransom note, or anything? And can I leave if I want to?"

"No ransom note," said Sam. "And you can leave any time."

"And may I have a full explanation?" Sally asked.

Sam stopped and took another swallow of wine. "Okay. Time for the full confession. I really did need some advice on Zambeziland taxes, but I could have gotten it from someone here. That was my excuse, to shanghai you into coming. I wanted you to come along with me because I never have time when I'm in the States to spend time with anyone, and I wanted to spend time with you. I wanted to go on a vacation and I wanted you to come with me. I figured you wouldn't mind doing London by yourself during the day when I was busy. I figured you wouldn't mind seeing the shows. I also figured you would begin to catch on to why I wanted you around. At least if I didn't push it too much.''

Maybe he doesn't have an ulterior motive, Sally thought, her heart beginning to accelerate. ''But why did you lie to me?'' she asked.

''Because I had to.'' Sam said. ''Because you wouldn't have come if I hadn't. Remember? You said so in the car.''

''That's because I'm not the kind of person who does things like this,'' Sally said. ''Alicia's the only one who thinks I should run off to England with a man. What will everyone say?''

''Everyone,'' said Sam, ''will say that you went to England with your employer on a tax consulting job.''

''But why did you pick me?'' Sally asked. ''The person who wants everything in order, hates spontaneity, the compulsive CPA.''

''Because it's more fun to pull surprises on you,'' Sam said. ''And you did fine. I expected you to read me the riot act a lot sooner than you did.''

''I beg your pardon?'' Sally said, nearly choking on her wine. ''You knew I was going to do that? I didn't.''

''I had it figured that there was a ninety-five percent risk you'd crown me with an umbrella and go home before now.''

''Only because that's an expensive umbrella,'' Sally muttered.

''So now, I'll tell you the full extent of the crime,'' Sam said, as the waiter brought the leek soup, and removed the pâté. When he was out of earshot, Sam said, "Look. I propose to spend the next week exploring the north of England, and Scotland. I have no reservations, no plans, no package. I intend to follow my nose and see where it takes me. Since it's off-season, there probably won't be any trouble getting a place to stay. I want to set your mind to rest. Remember, this is a very civilized country. You can drink the water, and there is good medical care available. It's not Zambeziland or Bangladesh." Sam stirred his soup. Now, he seemed to be having trouble looking Sally in the eye.

"I would like it very much if you went with me," he continued. "But you don't have to. I can take you back to London and have you on a plane out tomorrow. I want you to think about this for a while and tell me after dinner."

He took a sip of soup, made a face and said, "Whew, watch it. It's very hot."

"Sam, I'm sorry, but I still don't really understand. Why am I here?"

"I don't know what it is you want me to say," Sam said, stirring his soup. "You are here because I would like to get to know you better, and I don't know any other way to do it. I want to get to know you better because...well, I'm only asking you to think about it. While you are thinking, I want you to think about this. I know you are a CPA, that you never do anything on impulse, that my 'life-style' as they call it, horrifies you. In many ways, we're opposites. But think about how well you handled everything that I have thrown at you in the past week or so. You made it to the plane, new passport in hand, you flew like a veteran and even liked it, you digested the Zambeziland tax code, you managed to enjoy yourself in London all by yourself, with no prior planning—in fact, you seemed to be enjoying doing it that way. So think hard about this. I'd really like you to come along with me, but if you feel even slightly uncomfortable about it, don't. I don't want to make you unhappy. That's because I think I... well, never mind why. Now, eat your soup."

"What were you about to tell me just then?" Sally prompted.

"I think I was about to tell you a story I heard at Barclay's about one of the British football teams," Sam said with his crooked grin. "It seems that the fans, who get pretty wild over here, were..."

Chapter Five

Cold and dripping wet, even with vigilant use of umbrellas, Sally and Sam blew in the door of the bed and breakfast—or B and B, as Sally had learned they were called—into the floral-carpeted hall. Sam closed the door, took Sally's umbrella and his own and hung them on the rack by the door.

"Now that you've decided to come along," Sam said, pulling Sally to him, "I think it's time we tried this again." He put one finger under her chin, tilted her head back and looked long and deep into her eyes. Sally felt her entire body begin to warm and melt. At the same time...

"I've some 'ot cocoa roight here, dearies," said a cheery voice.

Sam and Sally jumped apart. A buxom woman, in a quilted print robe, with gray hair in plastic curlers and green hairnet, rounded the corner.

"You must be perfectly frozen," she said. "I've been waitin' for you to come in. The fire's still on in the lounge.

You two go on in there and I'll bring the cocoa. Can't 'ave me guests gettin' the ague."

"Thanks, Mrs. Musgrove," said Sam.

"That would be lovely," said Sally, with a faint sigh.

Later, lying in the narrow but warm and comfortable bed, watching the swaying tree branches silhouetted against the nearly full moon, Sally almost, but not quite, laughed. Mrs. Musgrove had brought the cocoa into the lounge and sat chatting with them while they drank it. Then she had followed them to their rooms, which were as far apart as possible in that small place, in fact on different floors. She had first escorted Sam into his, showed him the turned down bed, showed him where the night-light was, showed him how to latch the windows. Then she had pointedly closed the door on him and led Sally up the stairs, where she had gone through the same routine.

Then Mrs. Musgrove said, "You 'op into bed, dearie. If you want anything, I'm right out here." And with this she closed the door.

It was perfectly obvious, Sally thought, that Mrs. Musgrove was not going to allow any hanky panky in her bed and breakfast. Two people of different sexes and different last names were not going to get anywhere near each other. Well, thought Sally, perhaps it was just as well. She was rattled by what Sam had told her tonight—she was pleased and scared. Scared half to death, actually. She was heading into the great unknown. For whatever reason, Sam had gone to quite a lot of trouble to maneuver her into this. She'd found she really wanted to be in England with Sam. It was like flying—once she was on the plane, she'd liked it. Whatever the price, she thought, just this once, she'd try it—living the moment. It was very un-Sally like. Well, she thought, if nothing else, Alicia would be proud of her. She'd finally broken the mold.

And there had been no chance to talk to Sam, thanks to Mrs. Musgrove, dear soul that she was. And no chance to do what Sally now realized she wanted to do most in this world, since she knew how this was going to end up, anyway. She wanted to disappear into Sam's arms, feel his lips on hers, his hands moving on her back, then feel his mouth trailing fire down her neck, to her bare cool shoulders, then... Sally turned and groaned and buried her face in her pillow. As she did, she could have sworn she heard Mrs. Musgrove's heavy step outside in the hall.

Sam on the floor below Sally's definitely heard Mrs. Musgrove's footsteps over his head. He was lying on his back, arms crossed behind his head, staring out the window at the street lamp. Mrs. Musgrove amused him now, though a few minutes ago, he would have cheerfully strangled her.

He wasn't sleepy at all, despite the cocoa, and the heavy dinner and the wine.

So he thought about Sally. Sally who became more complex every day. He'd known all along that efficient exterior of hers was compensation for some fear deep inside. Someone had hurt Sally Forbes a great deal. He knew he had to break through that compulsiveness to reach the person beneath. The alcoholic father was a big part of it. He knew the effect alcoholics had on their families—children of alcoholics didn't dare trust anyone. He'd seen it before. Another part of it was years of habit, years of building a shell against the world. But he'd quickly found that his usual absent-minded high-handedness, his apparent disorganization—much of which was put on—worked. He had been delighted to see her fear of flying drop away. That was symbolic of what lay ahead, he thought. Sally, despite herself, was living hour by hour, minute by minute, and, he thought, enjoying it. Of course, luxury hotels, fine meals and London theater were easy to enjoy. He liked them, too. It might be different somewhere else.

But, and this was a big but, he'd kissed her, just once. Wrong time, wrong place, but it sure as hell was the right person. Before that, his interest in her had been a middling case of lust tempered with appreciation of her fragility and quirkiness. Something strange had happened to Sam that night. That kiss had done him in, in some way that was unfamiliar to him. So he had, more or less, laughed it off and kept his hands off her, much as he would have liked it otherwise. He had to figure out where this thing was going, and where he wanted it to go. But there was more to it than that. He couldn't tell how she felt about him, which mattered a lot. She seemed to like him, she laughed at all the right places, but whenever he got too close, she froze up and backed him off. Like the time he found out about her alcoholic father. So he backed off for his sake. For her sake. For everybody's sake.

Crash!

The shutter outside had blown loose, and Sam had to get out from under the warm covers and open the window and fasten it again. Then he had to assure Mrs. Musgrove who tapped anxiously at his door that the shutter was permanently anchored for the night. Sam crawled back into bed between the now-chilly sheets and made a concerted effort to go to sleep.

And failed. Sally kept bobbing up in his mind, like a fishing float. So Sam thought some more. He realized that he had pushed her too far, and that had resulted in her outburst in the car. He couldn't blame her. It was his fault. Then he explained it all to her, even though she was slow to catch on. She obviously needed reassurance, and he hadn't been able to give it to her, at least in the form she wanted. What he hadn't explained was how he felt about her. He couldn't, yet, because he didn't know what to do about it himself. You couldn't start defining feelings and futures until you knew what to do about it. And Sam was only beginning to know how he felt, much less what to do. And he was pretty sure that Sally didn't feel the same way about him. But he decided, he was in luck. She didn't trust him, he knew that, but she'd agreed to go along. That was a victory in itself.

He smiled. Everyone thought Sam Thatcher made instant decisions, picked his magic numbers out of the air. They thought that statements like, "There is a ninety percent chance South Africa will take control of any diamond mining operation in Zambeziland within six months of its inception" were floating around out there, somewhere, for him to grab. Boy, were they wrong. Years of accumulating data, thousands of questions, weeks of reading had gone into that simple sentence. And it would be right, because Sam took no risks with his risk estimates. The actual figure in Zambeziland was 100% in three months, but he had hedged. Now he had a problem, one in which he didn't have years of data, weeks of reading, thousands of questions answered, and he was uncomfortable. He was going to have to make a decision soon, come up with some personal risk estimates, and he didn't have enough data. That decision, of course, involved Sally.

He'd figured that night, in that eight-hundred-year-old house where they were staying, with the winter wind howling at the eaves, in a warm and cozy room with bright chintz and low lights, they'd both find out a few things about how they felt about each other. He would have taken that slender form in his arms, kissed those eyelids with the dark lashes, paused a long time to explore that warm mouth, and then, touching...

"Damn Mrs. Musgrove," said Sam, under his breath, pulling the pillow over his face.

The wind was so gusty that Sam was having trouble holding even the aerodynamically perfect Jaguar on the road. But then, it wasn't much of a road—just a narrow strip of black asphalt—or as the Brits would have it, bitumen—between two ancient stone walls. Sally was trying to read the hand-drawn map given to them by another guest at Mrs. Musgrove's, with little success.

"We take a little side road from Haltwhistle to Kirkwhelpington," she said, "but he didn't put a number on it, and I can't find a sign for either place."

Sam said, "From where to where?"

"Haltwhistle to Kirkwhelpington," said Sally. "And that's the truth."

"If I lived in a town called Haltwhistle or Kirkwhelpington, I wouldn't put up a sign, either," said Sam. "I have good news and bad news."

"What's that?"

"The bad news is that we're lost, and the good news is that it doesn't make any difference. All these towns look exactly alike."

Sally laughed. And then thought, a week ago, if somebody'd told me I'd be lost somewhere in the north of England, I'd have panicked. Now it's kind of fun. And the towns that looked exactly alike were wonderfully old and wonderfully picturesque, and the inhabitants seemed pleased and surprised to see them.

Sam had stopped the car in the middle of the empty road and was looking at the long ridge in the distance. "It's just amazing. It's got to be up on those hills, but I can't get there. All my life I've wanted to see Hadrian's Wall, and the damn thing runs all the way across England, and I can't find it."

"We can ask that man over there," Sally said.

"No more asking the natives," Sam said lugubriously. "Doesn't do a bit of good. It's the accent around here. Can't understand a word."

"Now you know how I felt at the airport," Sally said, smiling and starting to feel really good about this. Sam and his nose-following didn't always work out.

"Wipe that grin off your face," Sam growled. He reached over and tousled her hair. "So I can't find a seventy-three mile long wall. Or understand English. Minor failings. Otherwise, I'm perfect."

"So you keep telling me," said Sally. "What about your taxes?"

"Can we make a rule? That we never mention that word again on this trip?"

"Don't you find making rules like that taxing?" Sally said innocently.

"I'll get you for that, Sacajawea," said Sam. "Now it's your turn. Where do you want to go get lost?"

"We Indians never get lost, white man," Sally said. "We have real maps."

She pulled out the brochures she had collected at the Durham Tourist Information Centre, shuffled through them and read aloud, "Lindisfgarne—evocative ruins of a Benedictine priory, famed as the birthplace of Christianity in Britain. Founded in 635 A.D."

"Sounds interesting. How do we get there?"

"You're going to love this—it's your kind of thing. 'Located on Holy Island two miles off the Northumberland Coast.'"

"On an island two miles off the Northumberland Coast?" Sam exclaimed. "Doesn't that present a difficulty, or am I wrong?"

" 'Reached by a causeway at low tide. Tide tables posted at each end of causeway', it says here."

"Hmm," said Sam. "Where is it exactly?"

"OS Map 75, ref NU 126418," read Sally.

"That's as bad as asking a native," Sam said, starting the car. "We're in Northumberland, that much I'm sure of. Maybe we can find the North Sea. It's fairly large."

As the Jaguar purred slowly down the winding walled road, Sally remembered the question she had been wanting to ask Sam ever since they'd gotten to England.

"I've been meaning to ask, how do you drive on the wrong side of the road? I can't even remember which side of the car to get into. You amaze me."

"A snap. Pocahontas. Just stay to the left, and hope the guy coming the other way isn't another American."

They did find the North Sea, but first they found ancient crumbling castles and walled villages and seventh-century churches. The wind blew in gusts, and the rain came in all forms from drizzles to torrents. The sheep huddled together, their black tails to the wind. They stopped at the most historic towns and learned that each had a similar terrible litany of dates: this abbey was sacked and burned by the Danes 823 and 928, sacked by the Scots in 1041, 1050, 1176, 1204, 1301, 1468 destroyed by edict of Henry VIII, 1537.

"No wonder the emperor Hadrian built a wall," Sam muttered. "And no wonder they built all these tremendous castles."

"Sacking and burning must have been the Scottish national sport," said Sally. "Makes the Danes look like sissies."

"Careful," Sam warned her. "I have Scots ancestry. My mother's name was McAllister."

"Oh, I *am* sorry," said Sally.

When they found the road that led to Holy Island, Sam stopped to read the tide table posted by the roadside. "We have half an hour before it's cut off. We're in luck."

And he drove the car down the long narrow deserted asphalt strip across what looked to Sally like miles of quicksand. She tried not to say it, but out it came. "Wait, Sam. We'll get caught out there. We can't possibly get back. We don't know what's there. What if..."

"What if there's a Hilton out here?" Sam said, driving on.

Sally sighed. "I'm sorry. If there's a Hilton on Holy Island, I'll be very disappointed. I *want* to sleep in the car. Honest."

"That's better," said Sam. "Wow, take a look at that."

Holy Island was coming into view. It was low and flat except for a great rock that erupted out of one end of the island. Atop this rock was a fairy-tale citadel, a castle, silhouetted against the restless sea and leaden sky.

"Maybe we can sleep in that castle tonight," Sam said. "You get the dungeon."

"In that case, you can sleep in the moat," Sally told him.

There turned out to be a tiny village on Holy Island, with a couple of pubs, a store, two churches, and two inns. The castle being closed for the winter, they found rooms in the newer of the two inns—1785 was the date carved into the lintel over the door. The innkeeper was delighted to have guests, the only ones at this time of year, and in minutes cheerful coal fires were burning in grates in each of their rooms. The wind howled outside.

After watching the news on the telly, they went down the cobbled street to a pub to have a crab dinner. Some of the locals, fishermen, mostly, were there, and Sam drew them into a discussion of the Chunnel, the tunnel being built under the English Channel, and then learned everyone's opinion on Northern Ireland and privatization. Sally listened in silent amazement as Sam's careful questions on these highly inflammatory subjects drew out equally well thought out answers. She began to understand how he got his data, how he painlessly ferreted out information he could use somewhere, sometime. She guessed, for instance, that he might someday be asked for an estimate of the risks of investing in Belfast, say. They would be very great, even she could estimate that.

Perhaps, she thought, there was more method in his madness than she had previously realized. And anyway, it was interesting. Or sort of interesting. Her eyes began to droop. She lost the thread of what Sam was asking. Then she was in the grip of an enormous yawn. She tried to suppress it and could not.

Sam noticed the third yawn. Thank heavens, she thought.

"I'm sorry," he said. "I'd better take you back to the inn before you fall asleep here."

"Mmmph," said Sally, gratefully.

"Anyway, we'd better get back before the wind gets so strong we can't walk."

As Sam helped her back into her coat, he studied her face and said, "Are you all right?"

"I'm fine, really. Just tired."

But outside, Sally was instantly awake. Hunched against the howling wind, they made their way down the street between the dark ancient cottages, with their tightly shuttered windows. Behind the inn the eerie ruins of the Lindisfarne priory were silhouetted against a moonlit sky full of scudding clouds.

"Brr," said Sally. "This isn't an easy place to live."

"Think about it," Sam said, struggling to open the heavy door of the inn. "Those monks who first came here thirteen hundred years ago lived in huts made of wood and stood in the sea up to their necks for penance. And got pillaged and plundered and burned out regularly by the Danes."

Inside the warm welcoming entrance hall, with the door shut against the wind, Sally felt a rush of gratitude. "Thank heavens I live in the twentieth century," she said, and then she remembered the coal fires in the grates, the bizarre plumbing, the two-foot-thick walls and the two-ton doors.

"Well, maybe the eighteenth century," she conceded.

Sam laughed. "Well, I'm glad I'm not a monk."

Then he took her hand.

"Shall we go to bed?" he asked, leading her up the stairs.

Sally pondered that. Did he mean that literally? And if so, what would she do?

He led her to her room and went inside with her.

"The fire in here is low. Let me fix it for you," Sam said, adding coal from the scuttle and shifting it around with the poker.

It was icy in the room, and she had cold feet in more ways than one. She stood at the window, still bundled in her heavy coat, her hands in her pockets, and listened to the wind beat against the inn. Then she felt a tug at her elbow.

It was Sam, of course, still wearing his coat, "Let's stand in front of the fire until it warms up," he said.

He gently pulled her in front of the fire and slowly unwound her plaid wool scarf from around her neck. Sally stood staring as if hypnotized into the glowing coals and then felt his fingers slowly unbuttoning her coat and then his own. Then he slid his arms under her coat and around her.

"Look at me."

She raised her eyes.

The flames in his eyes shot her through with a warmth that no real fire could ever create.

His mouth came down on hers, and she disappeared as a solid entity of flesh and blood, and became only five senses lightly connected somewhere under her skin. She could taste the tang of the seawind on his mouth, smell the faint clean smell of aftershave and the salt sea. She could feel the roughness of his sweater against her cheek, the smooth warmth of his skin under her hands, and the thick hair laced between her fingers. She could feel the whole long leanness of him against her, through layers and layers of clothes. She could hear the rattle of the wind against the small square windowpanes and an occasional coal dropping in the grate. And most of all she could hear his heart, beating more and more rapidly.

He lifted his head and said, "You smell of the sea and the sand."

"I hope that's good." Sally said.

"It's wonderful," he said and then she felt his lips exploring her face, her eyes, her hair, and, just as she was about to pull him to her, her mouth. But his kiss was gentle, almost sweet, and did little to satisfy the rising impatience within her. When he lifted his head, she bit her lip. Seeing it, he grinned. She could just make out his face in the fire glow.

Then he slid his hands under her sweater and began a slow and careful exploration of the planes and curves there with the gentlest of fingertips, as if he had never touched a human body before. Sally's impatience began to turn to fever. Her hands began to reciprocate. But he had the better control, she realized. She peeked up at him through her tousled hair and caught a glimpse of that ghost of a cool grin. But then she put her head down on his chest and his heartbeat betrayed him.

The fever turned to fire, and even in her near delirium, she wondered why Sam's hands were not singed when they touched her. But he didn't seem to notice, for he continued the slow sweet kisses and the stroking until he had built a conflagration within her.

Then he looked down at her and said, "You're incandescent."

And something about those words broke the spell, caused her reeling brain to reconnect, to anchor itself in time and place. She stiffened. Sam felt it, for he said, "What's wrong?"

"I . . . I'm sorry, I can't go through with it," she managed to choke out. Her heart was beating so fast she feared it would fly out of her chest. Her knees were about to give way.

"Go through with it? I don't understand," Sam said, stepping back and looking down at her with a perplexed expression.

Sally took several deep breaths. "I can't . . . we can't . . . go to bed, with each other I mean."

She waited for his wrath or his laughter, or for some reaction that would show he knew how inadequate or stupid or silly or unsophisticated she was.

But he did none of those things.

He took her gently in his arms and said, "I understand. Things have been moving awfully fast. I think we'd be terrific if we went to bed, as you put it, but it's not something we're required to 'go through with.' It's no good if one of us regrets it in the morning, is it?"

Sally looked up at him and saw a great tenderness in his eyes that made her feel like weeping. "You understand, don't you?"

He nodded. "C'mon. It's time to go to bed—separately. Before I change my mind."

Sally lay in her bed that night for a long time without going to sleep, nor did she want to go to sleep. She was wide awake, but dreaming. She replayed the events of the evening, especially those last few minutes, on her mental VCR. Sam's kisses, Sam's touch, Sam, Sam, Sam. She could remember the feel of that long lean body of his, remember the way hers seemed to fit in just the right places, how his arms seemed to be just right for wrapping round her, and his mouth the perfect match for hers. It now seemed to her as if she and Sam had known each other for a thousand years. Why else would he have been so understanding about her desire—no, wrong word—her wish not to go through with it? Sally saw the word fear coming and instantly suppressed it. She was not afraid of sex or of Sam, of course not. Nothing like that. All in good time. Nothing to regret in the morning, as Sam said. Sam was right. Sam was a lot of other things, too.

Sally sighed happily and snuggled down in the warm bed. It really was amazing, the way she felt about Sam. They were yin and yang, light and dark, or—Sally smiled to herself—debit and credit. They were fireworks, thought Sally. Rockets red glare, bombs bursting in air... Stars and stripes forever, red, white and blue...incredible. Sally was sure that no two people ever felt that way before, not in all history.

Chapter Six

In the morning, Sally bounced out of bed, singing. She couldn't think of any songs about people named Sam, so she had to make up her own words and tunes. Sam, Sam, Sam, were the words to the first one. She peered out at the castle on the rock and the blue ocean, and the clean clear air, and ranged around the bright room full of cheerful chintz, collecting her bathrobe and a towel and shampoo and soap. Still humming, she all but skipped down the chilly hallway, with its deep red carpeting.

She opened the door to the bathroom. There, standing on lion's feet, was the largest deepest bathtub on earth. At one end of it were two small faucets, from which ran a thin rubber hose with a shower attachment on it.

Sally turned on the faucet marked "H" and after a minute or so a thin stream of cold water trickled out of the end of the shower attachment. After another five minutes, the water was running warm. Sally sighed, put in the plug, and went back to her room to get a book to read while the bathtub filled to a usable level. It was a good thing, she thought, that the inn was empty. What did they do when the ten or so rooms were full, and everyone wanted a bath?

Shivering a little, she sat on the side of the bathtub and tried to read. The book was an expose of CIA activities and was very depressing. It was an unfortunate choice of reading material, she decided. The water seemed to be filling the tub even slower, and the bathroom itself seemed to be getting chillier. Sally thought of Sam back in his own warm bed, and instead of a vision of skyrockets, a vision of the future set in. This wasn't the only place that she would be out in the cold, she suddenly knew. As soon as they got back to the States, that would be that—the end of it. Sam himself had said that he didn't have time in the States to see anybody. They'd go back, and he'd go off.

Sally took off her slippers and put her feet into the warmish water. It didn't even cover her toes yet. She sighed. What had she done? She didn't even have the excuse that she didn't know what was happening. She'd allowed herself to get emotionally attached to a man who was going to drop her at the first opportunity. Thank goodness, she'd had the sense not to go to bed with him. That would really have done it.

As the water level rose another millimeter, Sally tried to analyze how Sam felt about her. What had he said? Nothing, or more accurately, mere nothings. Your skin is like silk, you have eyes like stars in the sky, you smell like the sea wind and the heather. Recalling that, her heart turned over, and then turned instantly to lead. All very poetic, all meaningless. Anyway, if he was emotionally attached to her, wouldn't he have swept her off her feet and tossed her on the bed . . . like they did in the pirate movies? But he just said, *that's fine*. He didn't care even that much. In the cold light of day, Sally realized that she'd gone into this with a slight ache in her midsection and had come out of it with what they called in the old novels a grand passion, a magnificent obsession, that had absolutely no future. If only...

The water had reached her ankles, so she slid out of the bathrobe, and with a large collection of goosebumps, she stood in the tub. Holding the shower attachment over her head, she washed her hair, muttering at herself for her stupidity, and wishing she could cry. The water was now a respectable depth, so she slid down in the tub, stretched out full length with room to spare, and got warm for the first time since she'd gotten out of bed.

Ten minutes later, as the water was cooling off, there was a knock on the door.

"Sally, is that you in there?" she heard Sam's voice say.

"Who else could it be?" she said under her breath, "we're the only ones here." And then she raised her voice and said, "Yes, I'll be out in a minute."

She rinsed herself off, pulled the plug, got out of the tub and dried herself. She waited for the water to finish draining, and then carefully cleaned the tub. Then she put on her bathrobe, wrapped the towel around her wet hair, gathered her paraphernalia, and opened the door.

Sam was leaning against the door frame, wearing a terrycloth bathrobe and carrying his towel and shaving kit.

"Morning," he said, smiling down at her.

Sally looked up and was lost. There was a klunk as she dropped her makeup bag, and another as he dropped his shaving kit. Two towels fell to the floor, and Sam and Sally were in each other's arms again. Skyrockets roared to the sky, roman candles shot red, white and blue glory, and Sally was... emotionally attached all over again.

The innkeeper's wife fixed an enormous breakfast of eggs, bacon, chips, toast, orange juice and coffee, and Sam and Sally ate all of it. Sally had never in her life felt so hungry, or eaten anything so good. Nor had she ever felt so happy. She was almost afraid to look at Sam, for fear that she would do something terribly silly, like jump up and down and scream with joy. Sam, too, seemed happy, she thought, though he only talked of the most banal things. She could read it in his face, see it in his eyes. She decided she could live with that, with everything unspoken, as long as she was near him.

Over the second cup of coffee, Sam said, "Don't look now, but I think it's going to be a nice day."

Sally realized for the first time that it was the pale British sun coming in the window behind Sam's head, and not a halo. She looked further and saw that even the savage North Sea had a silvery calm. "The wind's died down, too." she said.

"Do you want to stay here another night? We can explore the island . . ."

"I want to stay another night," Sally interrupted.

So, in jeans and sweaters and windbreakers, with binoculars borrowed from the innkeeper, they wandered the island. They climbed a narrow path and hundreds of steps to the top of the citadel and looked out over the parapets at the sea and the fishing boats hauled out on the shore below for the winter.

"Good day for a Viking raid," said Sam. "Denmark's over there a couple of hundred miles. See anything out there?"

"Nope," said Sally, who had the binoculars. "No Danes, no boats, nothing. I don't see any oil rigs, either."

"Funny how things change in only a thousand years, isn't it? The North Sea used to be known for brutal raiders, and now it's known for offshore drilling rigs."

"Same thing," Sally said between her teeth.

Sam laughed. "See those rocks out there? Well, this booklet here says that when the monastery was closed the villagers had to find a way to make a living. So they did it by putting false lights out on those rocks and luring ships to their doom. Looting and mayhem have been standard operating procedure here all along."

"So this was *un*holy Island," Sally mused. "Do they still put out false lights? Or did they catch the QE2 and retire?"

"It says here that they discovered a new way to fish for herring, and the island became more prosperous."

"Sacking and looting sounds like more fun, now that you mention it."

And then they had to pause for a while in a long lovely kiss, as a private celebration of the fact that there were no Viking raiders, no oil rigs and no false lights to worry about on a glorious day like this.

After a while, they came back down to earth, at the foot of the castles, and wandered around the little bay to the priory. The priory was practically brand new. Construction began in 1093, and over centuries a red stone edifice of graceful arches and pillars and parapets and towers with slots for crossbowmen rose on Holy Island. The fortified priory did not fall to the Danes or the Scots, but to the edict of Henry the Eighth in 1537, which dissolved the monasteries. Now there remained only a roofless shell.

But Sally and Sam quickly discovered that they could figure out the layout easily enough, and there were many intact arches and passages and pillars and walls surrounded by a carpet of fine green grass.

"This is about the third thing we've seen that's in ruins because of that edict. Damn Henry the Eighth anyway!" Sally said.

"I'll bet that's what Anne Boleyn said, too." Sam laughed. "But these are good ruins. I don't see how the original could have been more beautiful."

"They're too good," Sally said, looking at a particularly fine arch through which could be seen the citadel. "Too picturesque, too romantic. I think we're in Disneyland. Like that castle out there—it's too fantastic looking. I think this must be a movie set. It's so beautiful and perfect that it can't be real. It's special effects."

"That's an odd way of looking at things," Sam said. "Why can't something beautiful and perfect be real?"

"Because," said Sally.

"Because what?" Sam prodded.

"I don't know. It's just a feeling I've always had that you should mistrust perfection, because it always masks a flaw."

"There speaks the pessimist," said Sam.

"Just a gut feeling, as you'd say," Sally said. "Let's go look at the church over there." She took a few steps in that direction. She wished she hadn't turned the conversation on this tack. It was getting painful, too close for comfort.

"Wait. I want to talk to you for a minute." Sam reached out and grabbed her arm before she could walk away.

"About what?" She looked up and saw that his brown eyes were very serious.

"It seems to me that this is a perfect place, on a perfect day, and that you are the perfect person to be here with. Where is the flaw?"

Sally sighed and looked away, fighting the rising panic. And then with a real effort she looked directly in his eyes. "In my experience, you often only see it in hindsight, but it's there."

"But you will admit that this is a perfect place and a perfect day, here and now?"

"Yes, but . . ."

"And you and I, here and now, if only in this one twenty-four hour period, are at least pretty good together, if not perfect?"

"More than pretty good," Sally said. "But what about tomorrow? The next twenty-four hour period? Or the next twenty-four days, or the next twenty-four years?"

Sam reached out, picked Sally up and put her on a pedestal, or actually on the base of a broken column, so that she was at eye level with him. Then he held her at arms length by her shoulders.

"Listen to me closely, Sacajawea. There's an idea I want to get across to you. There are a hundred ways to say it. Such as, 'Seize the day' or 'Gather ye rosebuds while ye may' or 'Take the cash and let the credit go,' which come to think of it, ought to appeal to you. How can I get you to understand?"

"I do understand," Sally said. "I know a saying, too. John Maynard Keynes: In the long run we're all dead."

"Keynes was talking about business cycles and the stock-market, damn it. That's not what I meant."

"Sam, I know what you mean. It's just hard for me, that's all. I'm trying to seize the day. I really am. It's just that I can't trust . . ." her voice trailed off.

"Me?" prompted Sam.

Sally shook her head. There was a long pause while she thought and thought, to be sure of what she meant. "I can't trust myself."

Sam dropped his arms, and Sally jumped down from the broken column. "I'm going over to the village church," she said. "I'll see you in a few minutes."

Since it was very clear that she wanted to be alone, Sam let her go. He turned and walked the other way, through the rosy-red arches until he reached what had once been the nave of the priory, and then around the wall that had once been the altar. From here he could gaze out at the sea, beyond the picturesque little fishing boats pulled out for the winter at the foot of the stunning citadel on the rock. It was, he decided, one of the most bleakly beautiful places he had ever seen in his life. And he had seen a lot of places.

And he was here with one of—no, not one of—the *only* woman he wanted to keep in his life. And he'd seen a lot of women in his life, too.

But something was badly wrong.

Sam considered taking a swing at the wall beside him. Then he reconsidered. It might relieve some frustration, but that sandstone would break his hand, for sure. He stuck his hands in his pockets and walked head down across the grass to the drystone wall at the foot of the rise. He scaled that, jumped down onto more grass and made his way to the cobble beach by the fishing boats. There he collected a handful of likely stones, and tried to skip them across the restless water in the cove.

After the first two or three, he got the hang of it again, and was very satisfied to get three skips—splash, splash, splash—on relatively rough water. The next one disappeared into a small wave. The one after that hit perfectly and skipped and skipped until it sank. Sam felt better. Ten skips at least. A really well-skipped rock.

He continued to pitch stones and thought about his relationship with Sally.

On the surface of it, they had everything. A good easy relationship. They did a lot of laughing and a lot of talking. They had similar vocabularies. And for him, there was an attraction, inexplicable, perhaps, but an overpowering attraction nonetheless. He thought it might have to do with the attraction of opposites—he needed some permanence, something unchanging in his life. But that, clearly, wasn't enough. There was more to life than a few burning kisses, good conversation, a magnetic sexual attraction and astonishing places like Lindisfarne.

There was . . . he still hesitated to use the word, even to himself, never having used it before, at least in regard to himself. It was called love. And it was irrational. But there it was.

For sure, that was what he was suffering from. He ticked off the symptoms: a silly grin kept creeping onto his face; he wanted to skip, not walk; he felt like singing and whistling all the time; he felt like climbing up on the highest tower of that citadel up there and yelling; he felt like grabbing Sally and rolling and laughing on that green—and soggy—grass. He felt like turning somersaults and cartwheels.

Sam tossed the rest of the stones into the water and made a bee line for the nearest grass. Then, glancing around to make sure no one was looking, he tried a cartwheel. It was a failure, but what did you expect from something you hadn't done since you were ten? He tried another. Better. A third was almost perfect, and then he did two linked ones. Feeling very proud of himself, he wiped the grass off his hands and looked up. Two Holy Island fishermen in their watch caps and plaid flannel shirts and dungarees were staring at him quizzically.

Sam grinned sheepishly, gave a half salute and walked down the beach, in the other direction, in a very dignified manner.

Okay, Sam, he said to himself. So you're a fool for love. So why don't you tell the lady and get on with it. Ah, there's the rub. Get on with what? The next trip to Diwalwal, Philippines, or Calcutta, or Cairo? Bangladesh? These were all on his agenda, along with Meeteetse, Wyoming. Garden spots of the world, all of them. None of them places for a CPA who liked things perfectly organized and perfectly predictable. Who hated risks.

Therefore, Sam thought, he could offer the woman he loved a little companionship, plus anything money could buy, a vacation in a safe not-very-foreign place like England or New York once in a while, and a few days of his time. That was it. He could not give her the things she needed most: permanency, stability.

She was doing a great job of faking it, pretending to enjoy this flood of spontaneity he had deliberately poured over her head. But her anxieties kept coming through, like they had on the road, like they had up there in the ruins of the priory. Most especially like they had last night in her room in front of the coal fire. Sam knew fear when he saw it. Sex, to Sally, was the ultimate risk. The words "go through with it" and "go to bed" when he, or anyone else, he figured, would have said "make love." "Making love" was so much finer and better than "going through with it." Sally was trying to be so game, he thought. He was almost sure he knew how she felt about him. The same way he felt about her, he thought, though she was afraid of it. In his arms, there was no question, but that was only one facet of it. He was sure he could read it in her eyes, in her face.

But there it was. He could get close to her, but not too close. By that he meant physically or psychologically close, but every time he got too close he ran into a wall of anxiety, and she pushed him away. As if he were the enemy, not a friend. And she had lied, up there in the ruins. It was not herself she did not trust, it was everybody.

So, what should he do? Declare his love, say that he wanted to love and honor and cherish her all the rest of her life, and then not be able to carry through? What would that do to the little girl inside her who had been lied to all her life by her father? Sam shook his head.

Seize the day, he'd advised her. Take the cash and let the credit go. Sam picked up a rock and threw it at the lighthouse at the end of the point, half a mile away. It fell short. It was good advice. Sam decided to enjoy his vacation and let the future take its course. Any declarations to Sally would be disastrous. Maybe later. Under the perfect circumstances. But not here.

Sam hiked back up to the church. Inside, Sally was looking at reproductions of the Lindisfarne Gospels, a magnificently illuminated calf-skin parchment book done in 693 A.D. by a monk named Eadfrith in "honour of God and St. Cuthbert." The original, Sally told him, was in the British Museum. The monk had used the skins of 150 calves, and the book had 264 leaves, each of which had 24 or 25 lines of handwriting. Forty-five different colors had been used . . .

So they stayed on Holy Island, in that strange and lovely weather. When they had learned every inch of the island—sand, sea grass, pieces of shipwrecks, and ancient mounds that might have had to do with the first monks, they ventured back to the mainland. Sam found Hadrian's Wall, finally. Then they explored the great fortress castles built by Norman families against the depredations of the murderous Scots. They shivered at names that reverberated down the ages: John of Gaunt, Duke of Lancaster, the man who would be king; Harry Percy, better known as Hotspur, first, hero of the Border Wars and then later, traitor to his king, Henry IV.

When they had their fill of the third century and the fourteenth century, they went back to the eighteenth century inn on Holy Island. Sally learned that a person could trust the tide tables, so the causeway didn't bother her. Sam regarded that as a small miracle. He learned that if he told Sally what he wanted to do in advance, she didn't always object, and was sometimes even ahead of him. Accommodations were being made; small changes were taking place. Each was pleased with the other.

After finishing his Cornish pasty one evening at the pub where they always went for dinner, Sam said, suddenly, "I've always wanted to go to the Shetland Islands."

The pub owner, and the four or five locals who were lifting a few and idly talking football, perked up and began to listen.

"Where are the Shetland Islands?" Sally asked. "I know they make sweaters and ponies there, but that's all."

"Here," said Sam, pulling out a travel brochure with a map on the back. "They're up there."

Sally stared. The Shetlands were closer to Norway than to Holy Island.

"Would you like to go?" Sam asked.

"There's an awful lot of water between us and them," Sally said. "Is there anywhere to stay there?" She started to say more, then bit it off.

"Ye can fly from Edinburgh," said the pub owner. "An' there's hotels."

"We're only an hour and a half from Edinburgh," said Sam. "Why don't we try it for a day or two?"

Sally's heart began to sink. She looked at the picture on the front of the brochure. The Shetlands appeared to be bleak, barren rocks far, far north in one of the most stormy dangerous seas on earth. She could guess what the trip there would be like from the picture of the plane. The aircraft had two propellers and looked to hold about thirty people.

"The plane only goes in good weather," said one of the fishermen.

"So we can go," Sam said.

Sally bit her tongue. The last thing on earth she wanted to do was fly on some dangerous little plane to some dangerous little rocks in the North Sea. A storm could come up

THE JOKER GOES WILD!

Play
this
card
right!

See
inside!

SILHOUETTE®
WANTS TO <u>GIVE</u> YOU

- 4 free books
- A free gold-plated chain
- A free mystery gift

GET YOUR GIFTS FROM SILHOUETTE®
ABSOLUTELY FREE!

Mail this card today!

PLACE
JOKER
STICKER
HERE

PLAY THIS CARD RIGHT!

YES! Please send me my 4 Silhouette Romance™ novels FREE along with my free Gold-Plated Chain and free mystery gift. I wish to receive all the benefits of the Silhouette Reader Service™ as explained on the opposite page.

(U-SIL-R-11/90) 215 CIS HAYW

NAME _____
(PLEASE PRINT)

ADDRESS _____ APT. _____

CITY _____

STATE _____ ZIP CODE _____

Offer limited to one per household and not valid to current Silhouette Romance subscribers. All orders subject to approval.

SILHOUETTE READER SERVICE "NO RISK" GUARANTEE

- There's no obligation to buy—and the free books remain yours to keep.
- You don't pay for postage and handling and receive books before they appear in stores.
- You may end your subscription anytime—just write and let us know or return any shipment to us at our cost.

IT'S NO JOKE!

**MAIL THE POSTPAID CARD AND
GET FREE GIFTS AND $9.00 WORTH OF
SILHOUETTE NOVELS—FREE!**

If offer card is missing, write to:
Silhouette Reader Service, P.O. Box 1867, Buffalo, NY 14269-1867

and strand them, or worse. Or the hotels could be full—of shipwrecked sailors or something. Probably the only food on the Shetlands was pickled herring. She might be allergic to Shetland wool and Shetland ponies. She thought of a thousand reasons not to go, but she still bit her tongue. She would do it for Sam, because he wanted to go. She was trying to seize the day.

But the pub owner said—to Sally's immense relief—"Ye shouldn't be fooled by this weather—'tis very unseasonable. A gale force storm can brew up out there in minutes. Ye could reach the Shetlands and ne'er get back. Unless that's what ye've go' in mind."

"No," said Sam, with a laugh. "I can't afford not to get back. I guess we'll stick around here for the rest of the week instead."

"In that case," said the pub keeper, "le' me stake ye and yer lady to a drink. Ye're practically natives here by now."

"Thanks," said Sam. "We accept. But tell me—is this relatively balmy weather really that unusual?"

"Well, no' really," said one of the locals. "We always get a few days of it around this time o' year. It can really fool ye. Newcomers go out in their boats, thinkin' the winter's over, and a storm comes and they're niver seen agin. Mark my words, ye haven't seen the end of winter. We got another month comin' at least."

The other locals nodded agreement.

The pub owner said, "Around here we call this weather false spring. All it does is disappoint you."

And for some reason, a long chill ran down Sally's spine. False spring. Traitorous spring. Like Hotspur, who fought valiantly for King Henry IV and then turned viciously against him, only a short six centuries ago.

So when they went back to the inn that night, they walked side by side, holding hands. It had not been lost on Sam that

Sally had done a lot of tongue-biting about the Shetlands, and the relief had been evident on her face when he learned it was too risky to go this time of year.

Sally knew that Sam had proposed that as some kind of test, that he was operating on some hidden agenda of his own. Sam was obviously aware that Sally still didn't trust him. Or actually, she did. She could trust him to take off in one direction or another—she hadn't quite expected it this soon. He was so restless that he couldn't stay a week in one place, she thought. That meant, for sure, that once they got back, he would head for parts unknown, such as the Shetlands. It was a false spring, a false relationship, for sure.

Sally woke in the middle of the night and could not go back to sleep. She tossed and turned, pounded the pillow into different configurations, practiced deep breathing, to no avail. She got up and went to the window. It was a beautiful clear still night, with the castle outlined against the moon, and the entire Milky Way leading to her window. She went to the closet, got her tennis shoes and put them on and then she put her coat on over her nightgown and slipped out of the room. She wanted to see what the priory ruins looked like by moonlight.

She crept past Sam's closed door and down the stairs and pulled open the heavy front door. She let it close slowly behind her so it wouldn't bang. Then she tiptoed across the stone walkway toward the priory.

She stopped and gasped. There was a dark figure standing motionless in the shadows. It turned toward her.

"Sam?"

"You're awake?"

"I couldn't sleep. What're you doing?"

"I couldn't sleep, either, so I'm watching for Danish raiders."

"See any?"

"Nope."

"Maybe the Scottish raiders are coming overland."

"We're safe. The tide's in, and it's a well known fact that Scots can't swim. Why don't you come over here? It's warmer."

"You're right, it is warmer here."

"Here's the way to really get warm."

There was a silence while Sam unbuttoned Sally's coat, slid his arms under it and pulled her close.

"Eeep! What's that?"

"My right hand."

"I thought it was an icebag."

"That's nothing compared to my left hand."

"Argh. Go away. You've got frostbite."

"And hypothermia."

"Hypothermia?"

"Yeah, my body temperature is down to about eighty degrees."

"That's probably terminal."

"Well, there is one emergency treatment for hypothermia. Admiral Byrd used it at the North Pole."

"Admiral Byrd was at the South Pole."

"Well, wherever."

"So what is this famous treatment for hypothermia?"

"It's like this: first let me unbutton my coat. Then you put your arms around me, and I put my arms around you. Thus. How's that?"

"That's okay. Now what?"

"Now move closer, like this. The more body contact, the more heat is transmitted to the victim."

"Who's the victim?"

"Who cares?"

"Mmmmm."

"Next, we do this."

"Do wha..."

Long pause.

"How was that?"

"Niiiiiice."

"You're actually purring, just like a cat."

"Prrrrrrrrr."

"Are my hands warm enough yet?"

"Umhmmmmm."

"Then I can put one here..."

Sudden intake of breath.

"And then there. Is that satisfactory?"

"Prrrrrrr."

"You're purring again."

"Mmmmmm."

"Ah..." said Sam, pulling away.

"What's the matter?" Sally asked, startled.

"Ah... Ah... choooo!" Sam sneezed. "Sorry."

"That kind of spoiled my mood," Sally said quickly. "And I think I've got gangrene of the feet. I'd better go inside."

So Sam escorted her inside and left her politely at the door of her room, but not before he gave her a kiss that sent skyrockets to the moon. She went inside and crawled into bed and was glad for that fortuitous sneeze, for she had been on the very verge of... going through with it.

She dreamt of handsome strangers in the moon-shadowed arches of an ancient priory.

Chapter Seven

It did indeed prove to be a false spring. The very next day a tremendous storm howled in from the North Sea, nearly inundating the island. Sam and Sally, on the advice of the innkeeper, left while the leaving was good. The force of the storm might make the causeway impassable, even at low tide. They regretfully said goodbye to the innkeeper and his wife, and promised—and meant it, at least then—to return someday. They sought out the pub keeper and wished him farewell, too. After five days, they felt they knew everyone and everything on Holy Island. And maybe they did.

Driving on the highway—the causeway and the island behind them invisible in the storm—Sam said, "I'll never forget Lindisfarne. I'm glad you found it."

"Lindisfarne in the spring. In the false spring," Sally replied bleakly.

"A false spring is better than no spring at all, Sacajawea," Sam said. He would have reached over and tousled her hair, but the driving was too difficult. The wind was blowing the Jaguar all over the road, and even with the windshield wipers at high speed, he couldn't see very well.

Sam, being determined to get to Scotland—he claimed that some of his McAllister ancestors probably made their living sacking and burning English churches over the border in Northumberland—drove slowly and carefully to Edinburgh, where the weather was still terrible. Sally's impression of Edinburgh was high dreary gray stone walls and a huge hump of castle on one side of the city, but it was seen entirely through semi-fogged up car windows.

At dinner, Sam insisted on ordering haggis, and Sally insisted on not watching while he ate it. She knew he was lying when he said it was delicious, and she put her fingers in her ears when he started a disquisition on things he'd eaten in some of the more out-of-the-way places in the world. All she heard was, "Compared to the fruit bats in Kota Kinabalu, this is . . ."

An orchestra tuned up, and, to old favorites interspersed with oddly syrupy arrangements of rock numbers, they danced and learned they were very good at it.

They seemed to be very good, Sally thought ironically, at those things that required physical coordination and physical teamwork. Probably would be great at tennis doubles. What a pity about the rest of it.

"Why are you frowning?" Sam asked, swinging her around grandly, Viennese waltz style, although the song was "Fame."

"Now I'm smiling," she said, putting her arms around his neck and moving as close to him as she could. But it wasn't much of a smile. After a while, the orchestra took a break, and Sam led her back to the table and pulled out her chair for her.

"Tomorrow we have to go back to London," Sam reminded her. "And the day after that, it's back on the 747.

If we leave early enough, we can get to London in time to make a big last night of it. A great dinner, a show, or maybe the opera. Would you like that?"

Sally studied his face. It was expressionless. That meant, she had learned, that he was presenting to her what he thought she'd like. Not necessarily what he wanted to do himself. So she said, "I don't know. Maybe just the dinner."

"I'm so glad you thought of that," Sam said. "Just the dinner. As a matter of fact," he said, "I've been doing a lot of thinking lately, as you may have noticed, and I was kind of hoping to discuss the results of my latest risk analysis with you. You know, as kind of a neutral observer. Do you think you might have the time to do that tomorrow night?"

"I think I could squeeze it in," Sally said. "Can you give me any hints?"

"Only that it has to do with seizing—or not seizing—days," Sam told her.

"Why not discuss it with me tonight?" Sally said.

"This isn't the right time or the right place. And anyway, I'm still gathering data. I have just a little more to get, and then it'll be ready for presentation."

"I see," said Sally. And possibly she did.

The storm had not let up by morning. The rain seemed to be on the verge of becoming snow. The drive back was dreadful. Sam's shoulders ached from hunching forward to see through the windshield. Somewhere around Newcastle-on-Tyne there was a terrible accident, and traffic was detoured around it on side roads. When they were at a dead stop in a line of gigantic snorting idling lorries, the rain suddenly let up, and Sam and Sally were treated to a view of total desolation. The detritus and poverty of coal mining were everywhere: abandoned collieries and decaying lifts, lines of squalid soot-blackened stone council houses stair-stepping up a hill. Below ran a polluted river, the water the exact color of toxic waste.

"Coals to Newcastle," Sally said under her breath.

A curtain of rain squalled in and obscured the view. The line of lorries began to move, and Sam shifted into first gear and moved the Jaguar slowly forward. Sally tried once again to get some music on the radio, but could only find static and a man's voice reciting livestock prices in a deadly monotone.

They pulled off M-1 for lunch in an ugly town they never learned the name of and ate microwaved shepherd's pie in a deserted pub, under the bored eye of a punk-looking bartender. Conversation was stilted, minimal.

Visibility improved as they headed south, but the driving was slow and difficult. Once when Sam had to brake quickly, he felt the rear of the Jag start to skid, so he slowed down even more. At this rate, he thought, they'd get to London well after dark. He had hoped that he'd have some thinking time to go over what he planned to say to Sally tonight, but this driving was too hard. He'd just have to wing it. He had changed his mind. He couldn't wait to get it out in the open. He'd decided to wine and dine her and then lay it all out in front of her: that he loved her, that he hoped she reciprocated his feelings, but...

He needed time. Would she be willing to wait a while and then see how it went? Or would she be willing at all? He glanced over to see her face. She was lost in thought.

Sally was thinking of false spring. How really false it was—those paradisiacal days on Holy Island in the spring sun, the sunsets making the Lindisfarne priory ruins glow rosy red, the great keep at Bamburgh castle with the sea thundering in at its foot, the warm and friendly dinners at the pub, the long moonlit evenings—all swallowed in the driving rain. The next glimpse she had had of England was that dreadful scene of destruction, those gaping mines, in Newcastle.

There are parallels in this world, Sally thought. Nature, or somebody was trying to tell her something. Holy Island had been perfect, no doubt about that, but she now saw the flaw in it, the imperfection. It was perfect because it was unreal. If she returned there, it would have disappeared. It could never be recreated. Like the weather, it was false. This, the long drive, the bad pub food, the terrible driving rain, and the empty coal mines of Newcastle were reality. Sam was part of the unreality, she realized. At least the Sam who had been on Holy Island. The real Sam, the one who didn't have time to pay his taxes, who was off in Zambezi-land three weeks out of four, the Sam who lived in a hotel room with a little loose change on his dresser as the only sign of his occupancy—that was the real Sam. No matter what he planned to say to her tonight, she knew that within a week, back at the office, he would have forgotten her name. And a few weeks after that, she would be gone, her job completed.

Sam was not for her. She had to face facts. The man for her wanted a house in the suburbs, two kids, two cars and a Labrador retriever. He held a high, but not too high, man-agement position in a Fortune 500 company, only traveled once a year, and took his vacation each year camping with the family at a national park. Sally would take five years off to have the children and then go back to work, with a great babysitter at the house. Later, after they'd gotten the kids through college and had the time and the money, they'd travel themselves. She'd bring her husband to Holy Island and tell him the whole story—that she'd been to England before and just hadn't mentioned it—about the perfect week on the perfect island, in the false spring, and how she'd decided that they were figments of her imagination.

She glanced over at Sam, at that craggy profile, and decided that she'd never tell her husband how handsome he was, or...all kinds of things. And then her heart did a kangaroo leap, and she gave an involuntary little gasp.

Sam must have heard it, because he glanced over at her and grinned that wonderful crooked grin. "I think it's going to stop raining any minute, Pocahontas," was all he said, but that was all it took for Sally to fall in love all over again with the imaginary Sam.

Fool that she was, the stars stayed in her eyes all the way to London. The rain did let up, and the clouds lifted off the hilltops. Sally's errant heart, the one that wouldn't listen to her head, was now so full of crazy happiness that she began to sing, in her awful off-key voice. Sam joined in in his awful off-key voice—another thing they had in common, Sally realized. They sang every song they could think of, except "Ninety-nine Bottles of Beer on The Wall," which Sam suggested and Sally rejected, and they pulled in under the porte cochere of the luxury hotel in London singing,

> "...the other side of the mountain,
> The other side of the mountain,
> The other side of the mounta-inn,
> Was all that he could see-e-e-e!"

The doorman who opened Sally's door and began taking the luggage out of the boot looked suitably disapproving.

At the hotel, Sam put a call through to Marcy in the office. Marcy was out for a couple of hours, he learned, and would return his call. Page me in the dining room when she calls, he told the desk. Then he called Sally in her room, where she was repacking, and said, "I'll come by your room in half an hour, for dinner. Dress up. I'm wearing black tie."

"Is the Prime Minister going to be there, or something?" Sally asked on the way down in the elevator. "Why're we so dressed up?"

"To match the food," said Sam. "This is not the kind of thing you eat wearing regular clothes."

"How do you know what we're eating?"

"Because I ordered it last night from Edinburgh."

"Oh," said Sally, but a hollow feeling was beginning to form underneath her heart. This, she knew, was it. Whatever "it" was. The end of seizing the day. The beginning of the end, or the end of the beginning. No, the beginning of the end.

Sally was proud that the other diners stared when the maître d' led them to the small private room at the back. She knew it was because Sam was so gorgeous. And she knew she didn't look bad herself. In the private room there was a table set for two, with a multitude of crystal glasses, crisp linen, silver including at least five forks, and with napkins folded to resemble swans. At both places was a handwritten menu in beautiful calligraphy.

The maître d' seated Sally, bowed and said, "The sommelier is at hand," and left.

Sally gaped at the menu. "Filo triangles stuffed with Herbed Chevre and Tomatoes, Baked Mushrooms with Brie and Toasted Walnuts. With two wines. Wow."

Sam grinned. "Don't eat too much, that's just the first course. I pulled out all the stops."

"So I see," said Sally. "Six wines, none of which I can pronounce. Sheesh."

A waiter arrived, bringing the appetizers, and the sommelier introduced, as he put it, the first wine. After Sam had done the obligatory sniffing, swirling, tasting and approving, the glasses were filled, and the waiter and the sommelier backed out of the room.

"I wonder what they'd do if we asked for catsup," Sally mused.

"They'd bring it." Sam advised her. "Don't you like this?"

"I love it," Sally said. "It's spectacular. This is kind of the Lindisfarne castle of dinners."

"Good. Because I want to propose a toast." Sam lifted his glass.

Sally raised hers.

"To us, and to spring at Lindisfarne," said Sam, and Sally felt just the slightest disappointment as their glasses clinked together. As she drank, she thought, what did I expect, anyway?

"Did I tell you you look lovely?" Sam asked.

Ah, that was more like it, thought Sally

"No, not for a while," she said with a smile.

"Well, you do," he said, looking at her long and hard. Then he picked up his fork, and said, "By the way, did you know that the European vineyards were killed by a blight about a hundred years ago, and that they were replanted with stock from the Napa Valley? So what we're drinking is really California wine. Under different names of course, but . . ."

Then came the Fettuccini with Smoked Turkey, Toasted Pinenuts and Caramelized Onions, along with two more white wines. That was followed by a cinnamon sorbet, to clean the palate, and then the main course, Petit Filet with Blackberry-Mint Butter, Wild and Brown Rice, and Fresh Green Beans with Dill. With a Haut Brion and a Margaux.

Throughout, Sam talked of wines and British politics, amusingly enough, but Sally began to be on pins and needles, wondering when he was going to bring up whatever he was going to bring up. The food was wonderful, even better than wonderful, the best she had ever eaten, but she could not get her mind off what was coming. Suddenly, the sickening thought occurred to her that he was filling her up with this great food and marvelous wine in order to soften the blow. He was going to say, *Goodbye, it's been great. And by the way, why don't you get another job—it would be really awkward having you around the office.*

"What's the matter?" Sam's voice came from across the table.

Sally looked up and there he was in all his glory, grinning crookedly at her. With a light in his eyes that was half concern and half... something else.

"Mr. Thatcher, your telephone call," said the maître d'. "In booth number two."

"Excuse me." Sam got up. "It's Marcy. I'll be back in ten seconds flat. Don't let your food get cold."

But Sam was not back in ten seconds flat. Sally picked at her filet and at the brown rice and took a desultory sip or two of Margaux. She saw the juices congealing on Sam's plate and signaled the waiter, who took it away someplace to keep it warm. The green beans lost their pizzazz and dropped off the fork. Sally tapped her foot, yawned, drummed her fingers, tried to refold her napkin into a swan. She got up, peeked out through the dining room, but could see nothing. How like the real Sam, she thought, to disappear like that in the middle of dinner. The immediate emotion that she felt was impatience, and that began to lap over into anger.

"May I bring you something, Madam?" asked the waiter, appearing at her elbow like magic.

"No, thank you," said Sally, though she wanted to say, "Bring me Sam Thatcher's head on a platter."

She fidgeted some more, counted to a hundred, did multiplication tables in her head. She sipped some more Margaux. She drew lines in the tablecloth with her fingernail. She took a mouthful of cold wild rice. Ugh.

And then Sam came back, his face like a thundercloud.

He sat down and took a hefty swig of wine. Then he reached across the table and took Sally's hands.

"Something came up while we were on Holy Island. I have to go to Singapore and I have to leave tonight. My plane leaves Heathrow at midnight, and I have to be there two hours early. That means I have to leave the hotel in less than an hour."

Sally sat in stunned silence.

"Will you be okay?" Sam asked.

Sally wanted to say, "I'll never be okay again," but nothing would come out. She nodded.

"By that I mean can you get on that flight tomorrow by yourself?"

"Of course," Sally said, finding her voice at last.

"I'm really sorry," said Sam. "You don't know how sorry I am about this. I..."

"Don't be sorry," said Sally. "It's your job and you have to do it. I understand. I have to do mine, too."

"I wouldn't go, except that it's very important. The man who wants to see me is..."

"Very important. I can guess that."

"This didn't turn out the way I planned it," Sam said. "I wanted to have this fabulous dinner, and then tell you...ask you...some things...and..."

Sally noticed for the first time since she had known him that Sam was having trouble getting his words out. She pulled her hands back and put them on her lap. She began to regret wearing this backless black dress. She was beginning to feel chilly. Exposed.

"I'll be back from Singapore in a week. We'll talk then."

"Sure," said Sally, looking fixedly at a point on the striped wallpaper just over Sam's left shoulder.

"Come back up to the room with me," Sam said, sounding more like his usual self. "Keep me company."

"No," said Sally. "I want to finish this wonderful dinner."

Sam stood up. "Okay. I'll bring your return ticket to you here. I'll take care of the hotel bill tonight. And you'll need some cash to get home from the airport ..."

"I have plenty of cash," said Sally.

When Sam had left, Sally told the waiter that Mr. Thatcher would not be coming back for the rest of the meal.

She was surprised to find that she could finish the entire salad of Mixed Garden Greens with Lemon-Thyme Vinaigrette, and make quite a dent in the Blueberry Cheesecake. The Gewurztraminer was too sweet. What a waste, she thought, looking at the devastation around her. Six bottles of barely touched wine, for instance. How silly. She tied a knot in her napkin, put it down on the table, leaned back in her chair, crossed her arms and waited for Sam.

When he arrived, wearing a suit, he handed her her ticket. "Be there two hours early, and go to the first class lounge," he said. "They'll take good care of you."

He put his hand out, as if to help her to her feet, but Sally ignored it.

"Well, then, we'll do it your way," he said, and he leaned over and kissed her, awkwardly.

She turned her head away, and he straightened.

"I'll see you in a week," he said.

Without looking at him, Sally said, "In a week, I should have the next batch of taxes ready."

* * *

In the room, Sally cried herself to sleep. In the morning, she was packed and ready to go so early that she toyed with the idea of taking the Underground to the airport. But it required changing trains three times, and she was afraid of getting lost, so she took a taxi instead. She sat in the first class lounge for three hours, leaving only to go to the newsstand to buy a six-hundred page barnburner of an adventure novel to read on the plane. The newspapers and business magazines available in the lounge all reminded her of Sam.

The flight was without incident and on time. The movies were not very good, and the instant cheerful service was annoying, Sally decided. She buried her nose in the book she had bought and tried to ignore the murmurs and giggles of the young honeymooners who sat with their heads together in the seats in front of her. She hardly realized she was in the air.

Under the first-in, last-off principle, her bag didn't come out on the carousel until almost the end. She had nothing to declare to Customs, and Immigration waved her through. She took the Shuttle to town, and a taxi to her apartment, hauled her single bag up two flights, and let herself in.

There was a note for her in the middle of the living room floor. It read,

Welcome home!!!! There's something wrong with your philodendron. It looks sick. I found a leak under the sink, so I turned the water off, but it ruined everything underneath. And you have a mouse, or mice. Other than that, everything's fine. I can't wait to hear about London. Call me soonest.

Alicia.

* * *

As Sam's plane was taking off from a refueling stop at Karachi, Sam was deciding he was not going to be in very good shape for his meeting tomorrow—or was it today? Normally, he could sleep like a hibernating bear on these long flights, but he hadn't been able to even doze on this one. Furthermore, he had the wrong clothes with him. Suits for the U. K. winter weren't right for Singapore, which persisted in sitting right on the equator twelve months out of the year. Damn, he thought. The first thing he'd have to do was go out and buy some clothes.

The reason he couldn't sleep, naturally, was Sally. As soon as she'd heard he had to leave, those shutters over her eyes had slammed down. She'd reverted to CPA on the spot. She'd been doing it all day. He'd learned to read it in her face, in her voice. She was expecting rejection, even asking for it. She cast him—or anyone else—as the alcoholic parent, breaking promises. Maybe he shouldn't have done the big buildup, the dinner with six wines, the I'll-save-it-for-tomorrow surprise, because it certainly backfired when he couldn't carry through. But that was part of the problem, maybe even was the problem.

Surely the professional side of Sally could understand that there were certain obligations, certain people he couldn't say "no" to. Surely she knew that he had promises to keep. When Harry Lee, for instance, said in his perfect Oxford accent that he wanted to see Sam, Sam went. Because what Harry Lee did affected every country in Asia. A lot of his success, Sam well knew, was due to his access to the movers and shakers of this world, some of them famous, some of them unknown outside their own countries. While he hadn't explained that to Sally—he couldn't tell her who he was going to see—she should have been more understanding, more professional about it.

But she hadn't. She'd acted as if he were walking out on her, deliberately stranding her on a desert island. She didn't

trust him. He'd lived right up to—or down to—her expec-
tations. He'd followed her hidden agenda. Sam thought
about that for a while and decided he felt wounded and
misunderstood. He even considered trying martyrdom for
a short time, but he decided that wasn't much fun. He
thought about Sally some more, going over and over it as he
had before, thinking that if he cut down on his trips and
started living some reasonably sane sort of life, maybe they
could...and then maybe they couldn't. Maybe it was
hopeless. Neither could change. He was hopeless, and she
was hopeless. Mutual hopelessness. Probably that was the
attraction, Sam thought sardonically, and then he finally
dozed off and slept fitfully the rest of the way to steaming,
seething, glittering Singapore.

Sally took a day to recover and then after calling the
apartment manager about the leak in the sink and the mice,
and deciding the philodendron was suffering from old age,
she called Alicia.

"Hey, welcome back! What's London like? How did you
and that hunk get along?"

Sally was prepared for this. Her set speech was ready.

"London is terrific. Just like you've heard. I had some
time off and I saw the Tower of London, St. Paul's, London Bridge, Waterloo Station, the British Museum..."

"Whoa," said Alicia. "That's not what I meant. I can see
all that in *National Geographic*. What I meant was how was
London with Sam Thatcher?"

"London is London, whether Sam Thatcher is there or
not, Alicia."

"Let me try again. What did you and Sam do in London?"

"Worked. He worked more than I did, of course. He was
looking into investments in Zambeziland, and I advised him
on taxes." Sally very nearly crossed her fingers when she

said this, but decided to save that for any real lies she might have to tell. In no way did she want Alicia to know what had happened. Alicia would have an opinion on it and lots of advice, and Sally didn't think she could take it, not now, anyway.

"You're hopeless, Sally. Answer me this. Did you two have dinner together?"

"Working dinners," said Sally.

"Is that all? Nothing went on between you?"

"When it was all over," Sally said, "I flew back here, and he went to Singapore. Does that sound like anything happened between us?"

Sally was exceedingly proud of the wording of that statement. And it stopped Alicia's questions on that score. The conversation turned to other matters. In Sally's absence, it seemed that George had proposed to Alicia for the 134th time, and she had made a final decision—absolutely flat-out no, and quit asking. Alicia was going to join a health club where she could not only get in shape, but meet some new and different men. Did Sally want to join, too?

"I'll think about it," said Sally. "Meanwhile, I have a lot of work to do. I want to wind up this job as soon as I can."

Sally's first temptation had been to quit, but her conscience wouldn't let her. Nobody else the agency could send over could pick up where she had dropped Sam's tax mess. It would be unprofessional. Sitting on the bus, going back to the office, Sally smiled grimly to herself. Unprofessional. Getting involved with one's employer was the most unprofessional thing you could do, she thought. It served her right. That whole unprofessional interlude—that piece of unreality, that false spring—would soon be laid entirely to rest. She'd finish the job and go on to better things. Later, she told herself, after Sam Thatcher and his taxes were completely out of her life, she could really put on a happy face and talk happily about her time in England—the Tower of London, the British Museum, Victoria Station, Buckingham Palace and all of Tour Number 9 . . . everything except Lindisfarne, Holy Island. That didn't exist.

At the first opportunity, Sally took Marcy to lunch and quizzed her carefully about Sam's schedule, on the excuse that she needed to know when he would be available to sign the returns. She could avoid him that way. She estimated that by working overtime for a month, she could get the job in shape for the accountant that she was going to find and train to replace her. She had already called Acme Temps and learned that an interesting job was coming up shortly: being part of a workout team that was disposing of the assets of a failed savings and loan.

At lunch, Marcy said that Sam had intended to go to Wyoming or Utah the following week, or someplace like that, and then Bangladesh, and Aseania and Djibouti.

"Aseania and Djibouti? Good Lord, I never heard of them."

"One's in Southeast Asia and the other's in Africa," Marcy said. "I never heard of them either until I had to make the airline reservations for Sam." She sighed. "At least my geography is getting very good in this job. And I know the names of airlines nobody every heard of. Like Mabuhay Airlines, and DanAir."

But, Marcy said, Sam had done a very strange thing when she'd talked to him about the urgent phone call from Singapore. Sam had sounded, well, put out, she said. She'd never heard him express any irritation before about a sudden change of plans like that. And then he'd brought up his schedule for the next couple of months.

"He said, 'Put 'em all on hold until I get back,'" Marcy told her. "He never did that before. So I don't know what will happen. And I can't tell you his schedule, but I'll let you know as soon as he tells me."

"He certainly is unpredictable, isn't he?" Sally asked, thinking hard about what Marcy had just said. What did that mean? Well, one thing it meant was that it might be harder to avoid him—or easier, depending on what he did.

"I used to see a certain method in his madness," Marcy said. "At least he was predictably unpredictable. But this one has me really confused. That was a different Sam Thatcher on the telephone from London. Do you know of anything that happened in London that might have caused him to do that?"

Sally crossed her fingers and shook her head.

For an entire week, before Sam got back from Singapore, Sally was very, very happy. Her apartment was back in its original condition—with a new philodendron and no more mice, though the leak in the sink was still troublesome—and the job was going like clockwork. Due to the fact that her two assistants had been plugging away like troopers in her absence, everything was at takeoff point. Sally only needed to do the finishing touches, pacify the IRS a few more times, and set up the new system she intended to pass on to her successor. Six weeks at the most. She loved setting up systems; it was the best part of any job. She liked to envision her work continuing, humming like a finely tuned engine, until the end of time—or at least until the next major tax law revision. It was, she guessed, her immortality. Others left ticking timebombs behind when they left a job; Sally would leave a ticking clock.

She found herself humming at work, so pleased was she with herself and the way things were working out. Yes, she was very, very happy.

Chapter Eight

And then Sam came back.

Sally was sitting in her office, reading the tax code to check a small point, when she felt a tingling at the back of her neck. Absentmindedly, she reached up to brush off whatever it was—an insect perhaps. But the brushing did no good. Nothing there. The tingling continued. She looked up. Nothing seemed to be wrong. But a feeling of foreboding swept over her. She looked out the window, wondering if a storm had suddenly come up. It was still a bright and sunny spring day.

One of her assistants, Lou, was hunched over the computer, punching in data. He seemed perfectly normal, but Sally asked anyway,

"Lou, do you feel anything strange? Like something's wrong?"

Lou looked up, puzzled. "No," he said.

Sally tried to dismiss it and go back to the tax code, but the tingling continued and the words scrambled on the page.

Then from the reception area outside, she heard a voice, or the undertone of a voice, and she knew that Sam was back, and that the tingling was her early warning system. She swung around in her chair so that her back was resolutely to the door. However, Sam did not stick his head around the door as she'd expected. Instead, she heard him go into his office, and the light on the phone went on immediately. And stayed on. She didn't see him at all that day. Or the day after. Or the day after that. But the whole time, her neck tingled, and she was not quite so happy as she had been before. In fact, she realized that she was waiting for the ax to fall, like Anne Boleyn. Did Anne Boleyn's neck tingle for days before her execution? Sally wondered.

But then, the ax had already fallen, hadn't it?

Then, one night the phone rang, about eight o'clock. Sally was happily ensconced before the television, watching reruns of Cagney and Lacey—she liked Lacey's family life— and sewing the buttons on a silk blouse she had just completed. She grumbled a little and went over to answer it, sure it was Alicia. Alicia should have known better than to call her in the midst of Cagney and Lacey reruns, she thought.

"Hello," she said.

"Hi, this is Sam," said the voice at the other end. The identification was unnecessary. Sally had recognized the voice from the first syllable.

Her heart went berserk. There was a long pause, while she struggled with it and an inability to get her words together.

"Hi, Sam," she said finally.

"I'd like to talk to you," said Sam. "In fact, I need to talk to you."

"About taxes?" Sally asked.

"Of course not," he said. "I want to talk to you about us."

Sally took a deep breath, swallowed hard, and said, "There's no such thing as us. Neither one of us has time."

"I do now," said Sam. "I rearranged my whole schedule. That's what I have been doing for the last three days."

"Well, my schedule's full. I'm booked until a year from Christmas."

"Sally, cut it out. We have to talk. How about dinner?"

"I've heard that song before, Sam. Or that song and dance. I can just see what would happen: right after the salad course, you'd have to leave for Namibia. No, thanks."

"I really hurt you, didn't I?" Sam's voice was suddenly so kind that Sally almost wept. But she knew that was the same old unpredictable act—he would try one way, and if he couldn't get what he wanted, he'd come in from another direction. Well, kindness would get him no further than anything else, Sally resolved.

"No," she said. "Not at all. Now, I have a phone call to make. Would you mind getting off the phone?"

The next day, the phone rang in Sally's office.

"It's for you," said Lou.

It was Sam. Another dinner invitation.

Though it was more difficult with two people listening, Sally managed another No, without revealing the subject of the conversation.

Sally stopped answering the phone at home.

She took to sending forms in to him via Marcy when she needed his signature.

On Saturday morning Sally, dressed in jeans and a T-shirt that read, "Save the Whales," with a bandanna around her hair, was standing on a stepladder swinging a broom at the corners of her ceiling. She had looked up one night and been appalled that she had not noticed the buildup of cobwebs.

She had planned to spend the day doing all the ugly dirty jobs around the apartment: cleaning the oven and the stove, spot-cleaning the carpets, getting all the crumbs out of the toaster, getting the mildew out of the corners of the tile in the bathroom, repotting some plants, washing the windows. First she made a list, which she put on the kitchen table for reference. Then she had organized the tasks in logical order and laid out all of the cleaning paraphernalia. She began by spraying the oven with oven cleaner, setting the timer, and then had attacked the ceiling. Figure out a time line, and start at the beginning, as she always did.

As she got a particularly good, or bad, cobweb, the doorbell rang. Damn, she thought, backing carefully down the ladder. It was probably the building manager again, about the leak in the sink, which had not quite disappeared.

So she didn't look first, but just swung the door open.

It was Sam.

Sally gasped in surprise.

He walked in before she could shut the door in his face.

He was smiling at her, exuding charm. He looked, she thought, like a kid, in his jeans and a sweatshirt that read "Stop Acid Rain." He ran a hand through his hair, as if he was thinking about what to say, and tousled it.

Sally thought her heart would break.

False spring, she said to herself. Remember that.

Her pulse slowed.

"We seem to have different causes," Sam said, at last.

"What?" Sally said. That one word was a triumph of mind over matter. She ordered up the shell that would protect her. It was slow in coming.

"You want to save whales, I want to stop acid rain."

"Ha ha," said Sally, just like that.

"I guess you've figured out why I'm here," Sam said, closing the door and closing the distance between them by several strides.

"Sam, I'm really busy. As you can see, I have these chores I've been putting off around here. I haven't got time to talk." Sally grabbed the broom and went back up the ladder, three steps. She willed her shell to close around her.

She took a vicious swipe at a high corner cobweb.

"I have something I want to tell you."

She backed down the ladder and moved it to another corner, waving off Sam's help. She climbed back up. The shell was nearly in place. Sally began to feel in control.

"So what do you have to tell me? Nothing can make any difference." She swung at another cobweb and missed. She climbed down the ladder and started to reposition it. Sam reached out and held her arm so that she couldn't move.

"I'd prefer you had your feet on the ground while I tell you this. I'd prefer you looked at me."

"There are a couple of bad spots on this rug. I never noticed them before because of the pattern," Sally said.

Sam dropped her arm.

Sally refused to look at him. The shell was complete.

"Okay, don't look at me," Sam said. "I'll get this out if it kills me. There were some things I wanted to tell you in London that I never got the chance to say. Very important things."

Sally looked up at the corner of the living room, over Sam's shoulder. "There's a very bad cobweb up there. I wonder how I missed it." She was very careful not to look in Sam's eyes. She was afraid of what she would see there. She was also afraid of what he would see in hers.

"I wanted to say..."

Sally looked over his other shoulder.

"I haven't got time."

"This will take only a minute. Please hear me out."

There was a buzzing from the kitchen.

"Oh, I forgot," Sally muttered. "The oven."

She headed for the kitchen. Sam followed.

She had already spread newspapers under the oven door. She had a bucket and sponge nearby. Donning big yellow rubber gloves, she knelt on the floor, opened the oven and began sponging. A chemical odor filled the kitchen.

Sam opened the window.

"I really didn't know what to expect," he said, "but I sort of hoped you'd be a little more sympathetic to my problem."

"What problem?" Sally said, her voice muffled because her head was in the oven.

"My problem is as follows: I wanted to tell you what I felt about you. All along. But I was afraid to say anything."

"Why was that?" came Sally's muffled voice.

"For fear you'd stick your head in an oven," said Sam, a trace of irony in his voice for the first time.

"Peach pie," said Sally. "It's all over the bottom of the oven. Damn."

Sally scraped and scrubbed. Sam waited patiently, leaning, arms crossed, against the counter. Then when he realized that she had a lot more scraping and scrubbing to do in there, he went into the living room, took the broom and without the aid of the ladder, swept down all the cobwebs. Then he looked at the list on the kitchen table, found the toaster, unplugged it, upended it, and shook the crumbs onto a piece of newspaper. When Sally pulled her head out of the oven, he had just finished washing the living room windows.

"Why don't you go away?" Sally said. "I am really busy."

"I'm not going away until you talk to me," said Sam. "Where's the carpet cleaner?"

Finally, every task on the list was completed, in less than half the time Sally had allotted. Sam had even borrowed a wrench from the manager and fixed the leak under the sink. Sally looked around, trying to think of something else to do, but failed.

"Anything else?" said Sam.

Sally sighed. "No. Thanks, I guess, for doing all that."

"Now what are your plans?"

"To sit down and rest for a minute," she said, starting to flop down on the soft white couch. But before she did, she stopped herself. Her clothes were covered with oven grease.

"I guess I'd better clean up first," she said. "I'm sure you can find your way out by yourself. The door's over there."

She was headed for the bedroom when Sam stopped her.

"You've used up your last excuse. It's a beautiful day, and there's a park a block away. Let's go sit under a tree in the park. You owe me that much—after all, look at all the work I did for you."

"I can't go anywhere looking like this," objected Sally.

"You look fine, just the way everybody looks on Saturday in the park. Just like me. Will you come willingly, or do I have to drag you by the hair or something?"

"Neither," said Sally, reaching for her keys. "Let's go and get this over with. I have half an hour. I'm, uh, expecting an important phone call."

"You might want to take off your rubber gloves," said Sam with that crooked grin, as he opened the door.

Sally could barely manage to suppress the twinge in her midsection that his grin caused. She preceded Sam out the door feeling like a child on the way to a dentist appointment. The walk to the park would give the shell some time to settle and harden completely.

* * *

It was indeed a beautiful spring day, and the park was teeming with life. The trees were putting out leaves in a multitude of greens, the grass had resurrected itself overnight, or so it seemed to Sally. Crocuses were pushing up, daffodils in flowerbeds flaunted their lacy yellow trumpets. Fruit trees were beginning to burst into clouds of pink and white blossoms.

And everywhere there were people enjoying the warm sun and the sparkling air. Mothers pushed babies in prams, lovers walked hand in hand, children swung on swings, boys played pickup baseball. People lay in the grass, some reading, some sleeping, some just relishing the sun, with happy smiles and closed eyes. It had been a long winter.

Sam bought hot dogs and root beers from a vendor's cart and handed one of each to Sally. "There's an unoccupied corner over there," he said. "In the sun."

They seated themselves on the grass. Sally sat stiff and cross-legged. Sam sat facing her, more relaxed, but Sally could see his tension in his body language. The sun was on her face, which felt good, she decided, but it was behind Sam, so she couldn't see his face very well. She bit into her hot dog, which, like all hot dogs bought in grimy places, was absolutely perfect, and she felt a little more mellow. A sip of root beer, and she started feeling even better. Then she remembered why they were here. She closed her eyes.

"Now, where were we?" Sam said.

"Back at Go, I think," Sally said.

"I was trying to say some of the things I wanted to say in London when I was so rudely interrupted."

Sally looked at her hot dog, very hard.

"Sally, please look at me."

The mustard, Sally noticed, was mostly at one end of the hot dog.

Sam sighed. "Okay, I'll say it to the top of your head. Listen to me closely. I love you."

Sally looked up at him, her heart in her throat.

His face was deadly serious. His brown eyes were full of . . . she couldn't tell what.

"I don't know what you mean," she said.

"Very simple," Sam said. "Three little words. I love you. I never said that to anyone before."

"I know what the words mean, but what does it *mean*?" Sally said, idiotically, she thought.

"What it means," Sam said, as if he understood her, "is that we—or I—have to do something about it."

Sally looked at him, told her heart to stop its erratic tattoo, and said, coolly, "It was a false spring."

"Now I don't know what *you* mean."

Sally had to look away. Sam reached out and took her hand, and she let him hold it, but didn't return the pressure.

"I think you must be confused," Sally said.

"I don't think so," Sam said. "I thought about it a long time."

"A long time for you is five minutes," said Sally, though she knew that wasn't fair.

"It was considerably longer than that. I was bothered by you the first time I saw you. And attracted. I deliberately followed up on it. I started thinking about it then. And, after a few false starts, usually involving taxes, you seemed to be . . . bothered and attracted, too. In fact, by the time we reached Holy Island, I was sure of it."

"Don't talk about Holy Island," Sally said, trying to sound curt, but unable to keep a note of sadness out of her voice.

"But Holy Island was perfect," Sam protested. "We were perfect—within our own limitations, but I think we handled that pretty well. It was a dream."

"Exactly. Holy Island was a dream. It doesn't exist in reality. It isn't there anymore. It's gone, and so are the people on it, including us. It was too perfect to exist, don't you see? Now we're back in the real world. Reality, where things aren't perfect."

Sam finished his hot dog and crumpled up the waxed white paper it had been wrapped in. He shook his head.

"Holy Island was real, all right. It's still there. Part of it's here right now."

"They called that the false spring," Sally said. "Those few days. The minute we left Holy Island that storm came in, and we were back in reality. And when we got to London, in the middle of your dream dinner, wham, reality struck like lightning. Off to Singapore. Don't you realize that dreams never come true?"

"Sally, you can make dreams come true. This is the real spring, here and now." Sam reached over and took her other hand. She didn't draw it away, but she didn't respond, either.

"How?" she asked, almost plaintively.

"Well, you could start by having a little faith in me."

"How can I do that?" she asked. "Every time I begin to trust somebody, they hurt me. Why should you be an exception?"

"Because I love you."

"But you've already let me down. You went to Singapore."

"I absolutely had no choice on that. The man I went to see was one of the most influential in Asia. I couldn't say no. I thought you'd understand that."

"I do understand. I do understand that those people are important to you. And I understand that is your real life. That made me understand that we had no future, you and me. Everyone is more important to you than I am. They have to be. They all have some kind of claim on your time that I don't have. Whoever they are. You don't have to make them more important than they are."

She stopped and thought a moment. She wanted to say it exactly right.

"I also understand," she continued, "that if we went on we'd become... lovers, and that would be even worse. I'd see you once every four weeks, if I was lucky. You'd always be jumping on a plane. To see some terribly important person. I could never... count on you, except to not count on you. Five days of false spring on Holy Island isn't enough, Sam, even if I do love you, too.'"

Sally pulled her hand away and put it over her mouth.

Sam looked at her hard. "What did you say?"

"I didn't say anything," Sally said between her teeth.

"Oh, I thought you said you loved me."

Silence.

Sally cleared her throat and went on. "No matter how I feel about you, Sam, don't you see that we are opposites? That it won't work? That I'll always feel betrayed?"

A baseball rolled up beside Sam. He picked it up and tossed it back to its owner. Then he said, "I've devoted a lot of thought to that. And tried to do something about it. I started by cutting my schedule way back. I've got more business than I want and I can let somebody else in the office handle a lot of the travel. It's something I've been thinking about anyway. I have only a couple of trips scheduled in the next two months." He grinned wryly. "Prime ministers and presidents only, from now on. It took some doing."

"Presidents and prime ministers? Are you trying to impress me?"

"No," said Sam. "It's just a way of screening out the others."

Sally said, "Do you think that it makes a difference to me whether you take off in the middle of dinner to see a camel driver or a prime minister? The point was, you did it, and you'll do it again."

"Sally," Sam said, "listen..."

"So what does your new all-celebrity schedule have to do with me?" Sally asked.

Sam took a deep breath. "What I'd like to propose is this: that we try it this way for a while and see how it works."

"Try what what way?" Sally asked. "With you out of town only half as much? And what do you mean, see how it works? Is this some kind of experiment?"

"I guess you could call it that. Maybe you could learn to trust me. Then we'd have a real relationship, instead of trying to second-guess each other all the time. I'm trying to change. For you. I'd like to try to make you happy."

"Why?"

"Because that would make me happy," said Sam in a tone of voice that Sally had never heard before.

There was a long, long silence. Sally looked out over the park. She heard the good solid crack of bat against ball, and one of the kids, knees and elbows pumping, ran for first base. The birds chirped. Lovers walked, holding hands and smiling and staring into space. A dog caught a Frisbee and returned it to his beaming owner. The sun shone down, and there was a faint odor of blossoms in the shining air.

Then Sally looked at Sam. He was looking out at the park, too, with the saddest expression she had ever seen on his face. She was suddenly stricken.

"I think I'd better get back," she said.

So Sam walked her home in the sunshine.

At the door, he said, "Sally, you're lying to yourself."

Sally said, "I know that, Sam. I have to."

So, Sally went back to work and started on the new system she was going to set up. She found that the harder she worked, the happier she was. Soon she was very, very happy. The more she said it to herself, the more likely she was to believe it. She saw Sam occasionally, going in or out, and once she even saw him with the blond woman who looked like Faye Dunaway. She thought for a moment that she might be jealous, but it was so obvious that the woman was chasing Sam again—Sam looked exceedingly uncomfortable—that she almost giggled. She was hardly aware of his presence, though he did seem to be around the office more these days. Maybe he really had cut down on his travel.

She and Alicia started their weekly meetings again. Alicia remained suspicious of Sally's laconic answers to what happened in London, but eventually gave up on the subject in the face of Sally's stonewalling.

"I'm very, very happy," Sally said. "I think London did me good. It made me think about how lucky I was to have what I have—a nice apartment with a long lease, sure employment, jobs I enjoy. I'm really looking forward to that next one, the savings and loan one—financial security. I've done it all myself. I'm satisfied with myself. I appreciate that. You need a change every once in a while to realize that you are really living the good life."

Alicia looked up. "You're kidding," she said.

"No," said Sally. "I'm really, really happy."

"Then why are you twisting your napkin like that?"

Sam went to Djibouti. Sally looked for it on a map, but that was as far as her interest went. Her job was completed far enough so that she could begin interviewing her successor. Acme Temps had another branch that placed permanent employees, so she called up and put in an order. A couple of days later, she began interviewing. It was hard. They were all bright young kids, eager and willing. They were all dressed for success.

When she had found two who were equally qualified and who, she thought, could live with Sam's operational style, she found out from Marcy when Sam would be back and made a formal appointment with him. To her surprise, he was waiting for her in the office at the specified time.

They had a short businesslike discussion in which Sally said that she thought Sam should interview the two finalists, since he would be working with whomever it was, and she wasn't. Sam said he would leave it up to her. While she was at it, Sally got his signature on the last tax returns, and told him he was now straight with Internal Revenue. She and her team of two would be leaving in a couple of weeks. Throughout the whole discussion, Sam looked out the window, and Sally looked at the carpet.

A few days later, Sally had lunch with Marcy at Hoffmeister's, where she had gone with Sam. She kept thinking about him during the lunch and decided it was the place. She never thought about him at work. But, drinking coffee afterward, she remembered something that Lou had said that day, while he was punching things into the IBM.

"Marcy, Lou said that Sam wrote a big check to an escrow company. Do you know anything about that?"

"I guess he's buying a house. Do you believe that?" Marcy said. "I never thought I'd see the day."

"What kind of house? Where?" Sally said, astonished. "Does this mean he's moving out of the hotel?"

"I don't know anything about it," Marcy told her. "I know he hasn't moved yet. I know practically nothing about his personal life. Maybe he's thinking about getting married."

To her surprise, Sally's heart plummeted to her shoes. She reminded herself that she was very, very happy without Sam and she would be very, very happy for him if he did get married. He was a nice guy.

"Who's he marrying?" Sally asked. "The blonde with the Lamborghini who looks like Faye Dunaway?"

"Not her, for sure," Marcy said. "He literally hides when she comes around now. And there doesn't seem to be anybody else. Even the mash notes have almost disappeared. He hasn't been in the news lately. At least I haven't seen anybody, and nobody's phoned. I screen all his calls."

"What a mystery," said Sally. "I wonder who it is?"

"Maybe that's not what it is at all," Marcy said. "But he's such a different person lately, I wouldn't even try to guess. He's changing everything around. Sending Al and Jack on trips he would have gone on himself before. Told me to discourage any new business. Now he's buying a house. And he strikes me as being . . . I don't know. Sad, or something. Brooding, like Heathcliffe. Anyway, it's not the Sam Thatcher I used to work for. At least things are more predictable, if not as lively."

"I see so little of him that I wouldn't know," Sally said. "What do you think accounts for his personality change, or whatever it is?"

Marcy sighed. "I don't know. But it started when he got back from Singapore, after that London trip. You said nothing happened in England, so I guess whatever it was that did it was in Singapore." She put her napkin on the table and stood up. "Time to get back," she said. "Are you *sure* nothing happened in London?"

Sally stood up, too, and crossed her fingers behind her back. "I didn't see much of him in London," she said. "So I don't know."

"Well, I can stop worrying about it for a week or two," Marcy said, weaving her way through the lunchtime crowd. "He's leaving for Aseania pretty soon. He can brood on the other side of the Pacific Ocean for a while."

Chapter Nine

A few days later, Sam asked Sally to come into his office.

"There's something I need tax advice on," he said. "I need your opinion."

"Like Zambeziland?" Sally asked without smiling.

"No," said Sam. "I'd appreciate it if you would take a look at something and tell me the personal tax consequences. It's legitimate. An investment."

"Can't you find someone else?"

"Of course I could, but I'm asking a favor," said Sam.

Sally was suddenly ashamed of herself.

"It's about half an hour's drive from here," Sam went on. "Shall we go?"

Sally nodded.

Sam took the Expressway to a residential area almost in the suburbs, but still technically within the city limits, as he explained to Sally on the way. He took the Navy Street exit and turned right on Colfax. He pulled up in front of a big old clapboard house with a sunporch on either side, and weeping willows in the front yard.

Sally gasped. It reminded her of the house she had grown up in. She could even guess what the layout was inside.

"Well, what do you think?" Sam asked, after a while.

"Think of what?" Sally said. She knew it sounded deliberately dense, but she really didn't know what he meant.

"The house, of course," said Sam. "I'm buying it."

"It depends on what you do with it. If it's rental property the tax situation is entirely different from the taxes on a primary residence. The tax code is very—"

"We'll talk about the taxes in a minute," Sam interrupted. "Meanwhile, let's go through it. I've got the keys."

He opened her car door and took her arm as they walked up the flagstone walk across the lovingly cared for lawn. The front door had a fanlight and a brass knocker. Sally tried not to notice the feeling of his hand on her arm.

He unlocked the door and swung it open. Directly ahead was a hallway and a curving staircase leading upward.

"Notice the banister," Sam said. "Can you imagine how much fun kids would have sliding down that?"

There was a big living room with a fireplace with glassed-in bookcases on either side, and opposite it was a dining room with a crystal chandelier. Both had beautiful hardwood floors.

"I don't like wall-to-wall carpeting," Sam said. "We used to play games on the pattern of the Persian rugs, when I was a kid."

The kitchen was big and sunny and had a wonderful breakfast nook surrounded by windows with deep sills that just ached for flowers like African violets. From the kitchen the big backyard was visible, beyond the two blooming lilacs by the back door.

"Big enough, almost, for softball games," said Sam. "I think it would be great to have a gazebo over in that corner."

Upstairs were four bedrooms, a lovely old-fashioned bathroom with a huge tub, and a cedar closet in the hallway.

"The woman who lived here just hated to sell it," Sam said. "Her children grew up in this house, and so did her grandchildren. But her husband died, and she just couldn't take care of it. I promised her that it would be as lovingly cared for as always, and she seemed to feel a lot better about it."

Throughout all this Sally had said nothing. She couldn't. She now knew what Sam was up to. The only question was, how had he managed to pick out her dream house? How did he know?

"Sam," she said, when they were standing in the living room again, "why did you buy this house? I mean, this particular one?"

He smiled. "Simple. I grew up in a house like this."

"Oh."

"Now ask me why I bought a house at all."

"Okay, why did you buy a house?"

"Because I'm growing up," said Sam. "I want some stability in my life. I'm tired of living in a hotel room. I want a home and all that goes with it."

Sally looked at him with narrowed eyes. "Are you all right, Sam?"

"Yes, I'm all right. Are you?"

"I'm fine thank you," Sally said. "Did you buy this to impress me?"

"No, I bought it because I wanted it. But I'd like to know if you like it," Sam said doggedly.

"I love it, Sam," Sally said. "It's a dream."

"Like Holy Island?"

"Exactly," said Sally.

"Let's talk reality," Sam said. "Suppose I change everything in my life I can possibly change. I buy a house, I move into it, I rearrange my entire schedule, so I only have to travel a little. I'll do everything that ordinary real life people do."

"Oh, Sam," said Sally. "You don't have to do any of those things, don't you see? We just aren't meant for each other. You'd be miserable doing that. Remember what you said at Lindisfarne? Let's not do anything that anyone regrets in the morning?"

Sam grabbed Sally by the shoulders and said, "I love you. And I think you love me. What do I have to do to prove it to you!"

Sally wanted nothing on earth more than to walk into his arms and dissolve, but she had been practicing on her shell so long that she had perfect control.

"We've been over and over and over it, Sam," she explained. "You'll still have to go to Calcutta in the middle of whatever you're doing with me, and I'll still feel betrayed."

"You could come along when I travel, at least to the nicer places. Would you like that?"

"No, I'd hate that. I have to work, and I'll only be working for you for a few more weeks. No more phony business trips. I can't just drop everything and fly off. The IRS doesn't like that. I need more warning. And I don't like to travel. Your famous gut feeling ought to tell you that."

"Didn't you enjoy going to England?"

"Well, yes, as a matter of fact, but that was different. That was traveling first class. Luxury. Jaguars and big name hotels and tickets to *Phantom*. But most of the time you go to places like Calcutta and Kuala Lumpur—or the Shetland Islands. I couldn't do it. I know that."

"I see," said Sam. "So I guess I couldn't take you along on most of my trips. Are you willing to take any risks at all?"

"You're a risk analyst. You ought to know."

"I guess the answer is no, then. You won't risk anything on me."

Now it was Sally's turn to sigh. She decided that it was time to deliver the speech that she had been mulling all day long. Actually she had been mulling it for weeks.

"Sam," she said, "it's just not going to work. It's not your fault. It's my fault. I can't change. The way you live, the way you operate makes me crazy. You operate on your gut feelings, and I operate on figures and math. And we don't add up. There's no bottom line with us. I need security and stability, and the only place I have ever found it was within myself. You are a very nice person, and I have been behaving like a jerk. I should have told you before. I don't want to hurt you. I can't make you happy, and you can't make me happy, except in magical unreal places like Holy Island."

She took a deep breath and went on. "Even if you gave up your work and stayed home all the time, it still wouldn't work. I'd still be expecting that phone call from Singapore, from somebody more important than I. It's too risky. I'd still feel betrayed. Just let me be. I am really, really happy with my accounting jobs, my apartment, my plants and my friends."

"And where does that leave me?" Sam asked, frowning for the first time.

"As a friend?" Sally said, idiotically. She knew that was impossible.

"I think not," said Sam.

She reached out and touched his face. "Sam, I never wanted to hurt you."

He looked down, searching her face.

"I'll always think of you as...as a glorious comet that rocketed through my quiet universe, leaving a trail of stardust..." Sally began, heard what she had said, and stopped. Then she burst out laughing. "Ugh. I apologize. That was so bad it even makes me slightly ill."

Sam started laughing, too. "That was terrible." He held out his hand to Sally. "Let's go back."

He took her to her apartment, not to the office, and at her door he said, "Well, I guess I'll see you at work once in a while."

"For the next few weeks only," said Sally. "I've already accepted another job. But I'm going to train somebody before I leave. You'll never be in trouble with the IRS again."

"That'll be a relief." Sam grinned that crooked grin, slam-dunking Sally's heart, but she had learned to ignore it. The shell hadn't really cracked once.

Sam held out his hand. Sally solemnly shook it and then found her key and unlocked her door.

"Just one more thing," Sam said.

When she turned around to hear what it was, he took her into his arms, looked deep into her eyes and then lowered his mouth to hers. From somewhere far away flared a brilliant comet, leaving a trail of stardust across her universe...

Sally closed the door, leaned on it, listening to Sam's retreating footsteps, thinking about what might have been. Then she went into her bedroom, threw herself across her bed, and cried until there were no more tears. She knew she had done the right thing. And now it was over. She had thought that the end of *l'affaire Sam* would be a relief.

It wasn't.

Sally had trouble working all the next day and the day after that. She hired, absentmindedly, she felt, the older of the two candidates for her job, and told him to start work on Monday. She called the employment agency with the news, and gave the new employee the papers to fill out for Social Security deductions, health benefits and so forth. She did not forget to have him fill out a W-4 for the IRS. That was all she got done in a day and a half. The rest of the time she was brooding. As Marcy said, like Heathcliffe.

That afternoon, Alicia called and said, "Let's get together at my place tonight."

Sally didn't really want to, but Alicia insisted.

After dinner at which Alicia insisted Sally finish at least two glasses of wine, Alicia said, "Okay, kiddo, this is it. There's something going on with you, and I want to know what it is. I'm not letting you out of my apartment until you confess."

So she made a full confession. The two glasses of wine helped, and when Sally was through, Alicia looked at her and said, "You're out of your mind. The man's in love with you, and you're in love with him, and he's changed his whole life-style for you. He even bought a house. Evidently for you. And you blew it."

"Whose side are you on, anyway?" said Sally. "And I'm not so sure I blew it. But it's too late to do anything about it now, and there are plenty of things that make me very, very wary, like his gut feelings and his—"

"Wary, schmary. That's what got you into trouble in the first place, Sally."

"But . . ."

"But me no buts. Do something about it."

"I can't. It's too late. I already told him that I wouldn't take any risks. He knows that."

"Does it still seem risky to you?"

"Of course it does. He could always leave me. He will leave me."

"Only for Singapore, dope."

"That's another thing. He claims that all the people he sees are celebrities."

"Celebrities?"

"Prime ministers, he said. He's trying to lay another trip on me."

"Maybe he does see prime ministers, Sally. So what? What is the matter with you? Here you've got the man of my dreams at your feet, he loves you, you love him, and just because he has to travel a little, you're rejecting him. It's not too late. Sally, he's a keeper. Don't you know a keeper when you see one? Or should I remind you of George?"

"Okay. Okay. So he's a keeper. But there's nothing to do about it. It's too late."

"It's never too late," Alicia said. "Now read my lips. Call him."

"I can't. I don't know the number."

"That's ridiculous."

"I know his room number at the Palace Hotel," Sally confessed. "What is it I'm supposed to say?"

"Call him up and say you want to go to Aseania with him!"

"I can't." Sally started to feel the old panic. "Can't I wait until he comes back? He's leaving tomorrow. Even if he wants me to go, I can't be ready. Aseania is a Third World country. I've never been . . ."

"Shut up," Alicia said sweetly. "Forget all that. That's the old Sally. Just call him. That'll prove it to him. All he can say is no."

"But I . . ."

"But me no buts. Do it."

"I'll use the phone in the bedroom," said Sally.

Alicia could read it in her face when she came back.

"What did he say?"

"He said no," Sally said. "At first he sounded sort of glad to hear from me. Then he didn't. He was nice about it, but he said that he thought I didn't really mean it, and it was too late. I told you that's what he'd say."

"Well, cheer up. You do mean it don't you?"

"Yes, I do," said Sally, "but what can I do?"

"You can go, anyway. Get back on the phone and make some reservations now. Hand me the phone book. Let's look under airlines."

"I can't do this!" Sally said. "I have to work. I can't go flying off on a wild goose chase to some country I've barely heard of. They probably don't even have hotels there. I'm a CPA..."

Then there was a pause. Alicia was looking at her as if she were wearing a space suit.

"Oh, yes I can," Sally said in a completely different tone of voice. "Hand me that phone book. Will you water my plants?" She started running her finger up and down the yellow pages. "Here's an airline that goes there."

She punched out the number. "Hello? Do you have daily flights to Aseania? Can I get on tomorrow's? It's full? The next day, then. Layover at Tokyo, I see. Yes, I want round trip, return reservation open. Tourist class. Yes, I am aware that I could save a lot of money if I made this reservation three weeks in advance, but I didn't have three weeks' notice. That much? OK, I'll pick up the ticket tomorrow at your downtown office. I'll be using a credit card. Forbes: F-O-R-B-E-S, first name Sally. Yes, the card number is 4198 20..."

At the end of the conversation with the airline reservation clerk Sally remembered something. "By the way, please sign me up for your frequent flyer program. I think I'll be collecting a lot of miles in the future."

* * *

This flight, Sally thought, wasn't anything like the flight
to London. The leg to Tokyo alone was longer, and here she
was crowded in the back, not stretched out in luxury in first
class. She had foolishly requested a window seat, not realizing that there was nothing to see at 40,000 feet, or that she
would have to ask a couple with a small child to move every
time she wanted to get out. Not very smart for a would-be
frequent flyer, she thought. She stayed cramped in her seat
through the movies, and then tried to sleep, but couldn't.
The entire plane was dark, and everyone seemed to be
asleep, even the crew. Except Sally. She finally snapped on
the overhead light, and in the cone of brightness that came
down on her head, read her book. Another barnburner, set
in medieval England. Vikings were mentioned, but not Holy
Island. Even under these cattle-car conditions, she forgot
she was afraid to fly.

Narita International Airport, where Sally spent four interminable hours, was Japan's revenge on foreigners for its
defeat in World War II. Sally found that she was hungry and
quickly learned that a visa was required to get something to
eat. Sally struggled her way through quarantine, Customs
and Immigration, changed some dollars to yen, and learned
that in the time since she'd left the United States ten hours
earlier, the dollar had lost five percent of its value. She was
looking forward to Japanese food, which she loved, but
there was no place at Narita to eat Japanese food. She had
a cup of coffee and a stale doughnut for ten dollars in yen,
struggled her way back through security and immigration,
and sat miserably on the backless benches beside the over-
flowing ashtrays, waiting with hundreds of other oppressed
passengers, as multiple TV sets blared out Japanese game
shows.

* * *

Nobody was ever as happy to see an airport as Sally was to see Kerida International. After nineteen hours, fifteen of them in the air, anywhere would have looked good, but this airport was not only beautiful, but had a friendly feeling about it. The customs agents were trim, and as efficient as in Japan, but somehow more humane. They accepted Sally's "Nothing to declare" without frowning. Outside in the warm, humid tropical night, she quickly found a taxi, and on the way into the city, Sally caught glimpses of swaying palms and elegant modern buildings and familiar signs: Coca Cola, Sony, McDonald's, Barclay's Bank. So this was the Third World, she thought. It seemed not much different from the First.

It was midnight, local time, when she reached the Kerida Hotel, which was so famous that even Sally had heard of it. It advertised in *The New Yorker* and other upscale American magazines. It was considered, she knew, one of the great old tropical hotels, like the Raffles in Singapore. And it was where Sam was staying, or so Marcy had told her. It had a vast lobby with parquet floors and rich mahogany paneling and crystal chandeliers, a dining room decorated with eight thousand cowrie shells, acres of glass and brocade and marble and brass. Sally had never seen anything like it. But she did not feel like wasting much time tonight looking at it. She was very happy when the bellhop picked up her bags and hustled her onto the elevator to the tenth and top floor.

The bellhop deposited Sally and her bags in Room 1020. She had not determined where Sam's room was, but at this point, she was too tired to care. She would find Sam in the morning. For now, all she wanted to do was get some sleep. Even Sam would agree that midnight was the right time to sleep, she thought.

She stripped off her clothes and stepped into the shower in the beautifully equipped bathroom. She had never felt anything better in her life than the warm water flowing over her. Third World plumbing, she had already decided, was much better than first world plumbing, or at least English plumbing. She stood there a long time, almost asleep on her feet, and finally stepped out. Only then did she realize that the room was air-conditioned down to only a few degrees above zero. She quickly toweled herself off, pulled out her nightgown, brushed her wet hair and crawled into the big bed, leaving the heavy quilted satin bedspread on for warmth. She curled up, heaving a happy sigh, and closed her eyes, certain that she would be asleep in seconds.

But as soon as she closed her eyes, she was back on the plane. She could hear the hiss of the jet engines, feel the slight turbulence. She opened her eyes and looked around the room to make sure she wasn't on a 747. She turned over and closed her eyes. The hiss and the turbulence began in earnest. Bump, bump, bump across the top of the clouds. She decided to ignore it. She pulled a pillow over her head. The plane hit a downdraft, and Sally's stomach dropped with it. She threw the pillow off and sat up.

The drapes were drawn over the windows. She got up and pulled the cord, and then looked out the wall of glass thus revealed. She gasped. Outside was a balcony, with a café table and chairs, boxes bursting with flowers, and beyond that was Kerida Bay, its outline traced in city lights. In the dock area, freighters were being unloaded and out on the Bay itself were the lights of a hundred ships and boats at anchor. In the center of these was a brightly illuminated white cruise ship, strings of flags flying from its funnel. It was breathtaking.

Sally opened the sliding glass door and stepped out on the balcony. Here it was warm and muggy, a pleasant relief after the icy room behind her. She leaned on the balcony rail and drank in the scene below.

A voice very close to her said, "Well, well, well, what a surprise." Sally jumped about six inches in the air. Sam was standing right beside her.

"How did you get on my balcony?" she said, when she found her voice.

"It's my balcony, too," Sam said. "It runs all the way around the floor."

Sally looked at his shadowed face. She was not ready for this, and she didn't think the look on his face was all that friendly. She decided to take the coward's way out.

"Well," she said. "I think I'll go back in. I think I can probably go to sleep now."

"No," said Sam. "First you explain what it is you are doing here."

"Would you believe I'm taking a little vacation?"

"No," he said again. "I wouldn't believe that."

"Okay, I followed you."

"Why?"

"Because I made a mistake. I made a terrible mistake and I want to make it up to you."

"Make it up to me? How?"

It had all seemed terribly clear to Sally when she had been talking about it with Alicia, but now she didn't understand why she had done this. She thought and thought.

"You seem to be having trouble explaining it," Sam said. "How am I supposed to understand it?"

"Sam, I wanted to prove to you . . . to prove to you that I could take risks. That I'd take risks for you. That I'd go to the ends of the earth for you."

"Well, there are two things wrong with that. One, I'm working and didn't plan on anyone being along, and two, this isn't exactly the ends of the earth. Now it happens that

I am going up to a place called Torogi in a couple of days, and that *is* the end of the earth. Really risky. You couldn't take it. It's the Shetland Islands of Aseania. So, it does look like you came here for a vacation. I understand the beaches here are nice.''

''Sam, please.''

''Too late,'' he said. He looked at his watch. ''I've got an early appointment with the Prime Minister.''

Sally, who had been thinking that she'd practically spent her life savings to get here only to be rejected, felt rising anger. ''Prime Minister, my foot.'' she said.

Sam raised his eyebrows. ''You think I'm lying to you?''

''Well, I guess so,'' said Sally, ''now that you put it that way.''

''Come along in the morning and see, then,'' he said. ''See you in the coffee shop at nine.'' He walked off.

Sally went back into her room, pulled the drapes closed, and phoned the front desk to request a wake-up call for eight a.m.

She crawled back into bed. She thought about that conversation for a moment. Something was wrong with it. Why hadn't he been more surprised to see her? Why had Sam suddenly invited her along to see the Prime Minister. Probably because he thought she wouldn't go. Well, she'd fool him. She didn't blame him for being so cool to her, but she couldn't help wondering why she thought she'd caught a twinkle of humor in his eye. Or maybe she hadn't. Maybe it was her imagination, that glint.

She turned over, pulled the covers up to her chin, and closed her eyes. Instantly she plummeted into sleep as if from the top of a cliff.

Chapter Ten

In the morning Sally woke feeling fresh and bright even before the call came from the desk. She showered again and found a relatively unwrinkled linen skirt and a silk blouse, and managed to get her hair into some reasonable configuration. She had been in the coffee shop for fifteen minutes and was on her second cup of strong locally grown coffee when Sam appeared.

Sally tried to quiz Sam on what would happen in the meeting. But all he would say was, "Just listen. That's all I'm going to do."

"But what is it all about?" she persisted.

"I've been asked by a couple of large banks to find out if it's worth their while to lend the government a lot of money to build a series of five dams on one of the rivers here."

"But why do the banks need you? Doesn't the government of the country give them all the specifications?"

"Governments have been known to lie. And here in the Third World governments are notorious for being corrupt.

That's how a lot of American banks got in trouble. They loaned out the money, and the dictator and his friends disappeared with it.''

It was only when the long black Mercedes limo with license plate Number One appeared to pick them up that Sally realized that maybe they *were* going to see the Prime Minister. Sam assured her that she would not have to back out of the room bowing, or kiss anyone's ring. There was no protocol involved, he explained.

She was so busy contemplating this that she failed to see any of the passing scenery and only noticed when a pair of uniformed guards waved them through the ornate gates opening onto a long drive. The limo pulled up in front of a long low white stucco building with a red tile roof in an architectural style that Sally instantly recognized as colonial.

"This used to be the British governor-general's residence," Sam said, as another splendidly uniformed soldier opened the door of the limousine. "Now it's the palace."

"Palace?" Sally echoed. Gad, what had she gotten herself into. Then she thought of something: "Does the Prime Minister speak English?"

"Probably better than you and I do. He's an Oxford graduate," Sam told her.

When they arrived, through three anterooms, in the Prime Minister's vast and elegant office, it was worse than Sally had imagined. Not only was the Prime Minister himself there, but the Minister of Finance, the Minister of Foreign Affairs, the Minister of Interior Affairs, the Minister of... Her head was spinning with the introductions, and with all the elegant—and understandable—British English. Sam had called her "my colleague." She sank onto a red velvet and gilt chair and began work on her job of listening.

First there was a beautifully done slide show, with maps showing the river that was to be dammed, and architectural renderings of each of the five dams. There were artist's drawings of what the countryside would look like before and after the dams were built. There were long columns of figures about hydroelectric output, charts and graphs in many colors, pictures of power grids, and cost effectiveness formulas, interest rate projections. Sally could follow it, if she concentrated. It looked good, very good, to her.

She glanced over at Sam. He was watching it all with an expression of polite interest.

"So, Mr. Thatcher," said the Prime Minister, "you see the benefits these dams would bring to our country. We have six million people in the Kerida metropolitan area now, and the projections are for that number to double in the next ten years, as we continue to industrialize. These dams would provide all the electricity Kerida would need in the foreseeable future."

"Furthermore," said the Minister of Foreign Affairs, "Aseania has, as you know, one of the most stable governments in Asia. The Prime Minister has been in office twenty-eight years, and the ruling party holds ninety percent of the seats in parliament."

"The payback period," said the Minister of Finance, "would be less than twenty years."

"Do you have any questions?" asked the Prime Minister.

"No," Sam said, to Sally's amazement. Even with that splendid presentation, she could think of twenty things to ask.

Sam stood up, shook hands with everyone in the room, took the leather-bound looseleaf notebooks the Prime Minister offered, and headed for the door. Sally followed close behind. At the door Sam said, "Oh, yes. There is one question. Will these dams displace many people?"

The Prime Minister said smoothly, "Not as many as they will benefit. And the plans, of course, contain resettlement provisions. Anyway, the people in Sulu province are mainly backward tribal peoples. The dams will bring them into the twentieth century. That has been one of the longstanding goals of this government"

"I'm sure," said Sam.

In the limo, on the way back to the hotel, Sally tried to talk to Sam about what had just happened, but he shook his head and pointed at the driver. "Later," he said.

This time, Sally looked at the city as they hummed smoothly through it. Near the Palace, Kerida seemed to consist entirely of high walls, some of them with barbed wire and broken glass embedded in their tops. Through the occasional grilled gate, she caught sight of enormous modern houses and gracious gardens. Then they were out of the walls and into teeming streets full of small shabby shops and old unpainted wooden houses built in tropical style with the second floor overhanging the first. They seemed to lean wearily against each other. And here the people seemed to live on the streets in front of the open-fronted shops, which sold everything from newspapers to plastic dishpans to live chickens. They were behind an old red bus, and the vehicle behind them was a horse cart, Sally noticed.

There were ragged barefoot vendors everywhere, and whenever the limousine stopped the vendors ran out into the maze of traffic and offered their wares. And there were beggars of all descriptions. Some of them were very young children. Sally couldn't look at their eyes. Sam emptied his pockets, and then Sally did the same with her purse.

"Welcome to the Third World," said Sam, handing his last coins to a dirt-smeared little girl in a ragged pink dress who could not have been older than four.

At the hotel, they sat on a couch in the lobby, and Sally said, "Are you through now? Isn't that all you need to know? It seems pretty clear to me that those dams would do a world of good."

"Mmmmm," said Sam.

"What does that mean?" Sally asked. "That was an impressive presentation."

"That was smoke and mirrors."

"Smoke and mirrors?" Sally asked.

"A fancy presentation designed to be so spectacular that you forget what it's really all about. Smoke and mirrors. And what it's really all about is something other than supplying hydroelectric power to the city of Kerida."

"What is it all about, then?" Sally asked.

"I don't know yet. Somebody in that room today, probably everybody, is going to make a lot of money out of it."

"Why do you think that?"

"Because the government of Aseania is one of the most corrupt in Asia. And everybody in that room was lying."

Sally caught her breath. "You told me they all went to Oxford or Cambridge. Do Oxford graduates lie?"

"Better than anybody else," said Sam. "Take a look at the figures in those notebooks the Prime Minister gave us, and then take a look at the figures I got from the UN and the World Bank. I'll bet that they don't even agree on the population of the country."

"So you're going to recommend that the banks don't loan the money?" Sally asked.

"No. I don't make recommendations. I assess risk. And I have to talk to a lot more people."

"Who?"

"Well, first and foremost, those tribal people these dams are going to displace. They probably know more about it than anybody. Maybe they don't want to be catapulted into the twentieth century."

Just then a bellhop appeared at Sam's elbow. He held a silver tray upon which was a cream-colored square envelope.

"For you, Mr. Thatcher," said the bellhop.

Sam took the envelope and opened it. He smiled.

He took out a business card and wrote something on it, and handed it to the waiting bellhop. "Give this to Mr. Arafura's driver," he said, dropping a tip on the bellhop's tray.

"What was that?" Sally asked.

"That was a dinner invitation from the richest man in the country," Sam said. "He just happens to own the construction company that would build the dams."

"And he's trying to influence you?"

"Well, he won't get the chance," Sam told her. "I turned it down. Along with the invitation to the private island of the Finance Minister, and the invitation to play polo with the second richest man in the country."

"You're kidding!" she said.

"Now you know a little bit about how some of these countries out here managed to borrow so much money from the big international banks. The bankers came over here and saw that shiny airport, and this hotel, and those highrises, and met these beautifully educated people, and just opened the bank vaults. All of a sudden it turned out that the stable governments were disguised dictatorships, and the money wasn't going into development projects but into private pockets, and the loans couldn't be paid back."

"And that's the International Debt Crisis?" Sally asked.

"A lot of it."

"But didn't those bankers see those terrible slums? Those big mansions next to those hungry kids?"

"Probably not. Sometimes they just fence off the slums so visitors can't see them."

"That's awful," Sally said.

Sam stood up. "I have to leave. I'm going over to the university to see an old friend who teaches there. I'm sure he has some information on those dams."

"Before you go, I want to borrow something." Sally jumped to her feet, too. "I want to borrow those figures you've got from the UN and the World Bank. Also those notebooks you got from the Prime Minister."

"You're kidding," Sam said. "What do you want those for?"

"Because I'm interested, okay?" Sally said. "If I can't do anything else here, I can learn something."

"You aren't really interested, are you? This is what I do, not what you do. Why don't you go to the beach?" said Sam. "The hotel has a bus."

"Just give me the stuff," Sally told him. "I can amuse myself."

He went to his room to get it, and while she waited, Sally thought about what was happening. He probably thought she wanted the stuff to pretend she was interested to please him. Well, she did. But she didn't have to pretend. She was interested. That much was true. But she didn't seem to be pleasing him very much. He was treating her like a...child. Or worse. It was painful, but she would prevail. She would prove it to him. What "it" was she wasn't sure, but she'd follow him to the ends of the earth to do it.

Sam came back at nine that night and found Sally working in her room. She had been out on the balcony, but after dark had fallen, the light had attracted dive-bomber sized insects, so she had retreated inside. The remains of her room service dinner were on a tray on the dresser.

"Still at it?" Sam asked.

"This is interesting. Wait'll you see it. It's really shocking. Last year they claimed to have a billion in foreign exchange reserves. It turned out they had none."

And so Sally, outraged at a country that would cook its own books, went on and on about what she was finding, and Sam leaned on the door frame and listened with a tolerant smile. When she finally decided that he wasn't listening, she accused, "You haven't heard a word I said."

"Sure I did," he said. "Unemployment is either seven percent, twelve percent or thirty percent, GNP either fifty billion or forty-five billion, and I have a Rand Corporation study that says it's well below that."

Sally looked at him long and hard. "I finally begin to understand why you use gut feeling. You sure can't use figures. These are all imaginary."

"Like Holy Island?" Sam said.

"I should have said false," said Sally, quickly.

"Like spring," Sam said. "Well, I'm glad you're learning so much, but I'm going to turn in now. I'm leaving for the ends of the earth tomorrow."

"Where's the ends of the earth?"

"A town, or village in the mountains called Torogi. It's the most accessible of the dam sites."

"Can...may I go?" Sally asked, without flinching once.

Sam grinned. "I'm afraid not. You'd never make it in a million years. I've never been there. There may not even be a hotel, from what I hear. It's very primitive, very risky. Not your cup of tea at all."

"Sam, I would have gone to the Shetlands, if you'd decided to go."

"This makes the Shetlands look like that hotel in London."

"Sam, please. I can take it. I flew tourist all the way here. I've spent time at Narita airport. I am a seasoned traveler now." Sally smiled to let Sam know she was kidding. Except she wasn't.

"It's not your kind of place, Sally," Sam said seriously. "It's a long, hard trip. The accommodations are sure to be primitive. There's been violence there. Even rumors of headhunting."

"Headhunting? That's ridiculous. You're just trying to scare me off."

"That's right, I am," Sam said. "You can't go along."

To Sally, he looked implacable. She sighed. "When will you be back?"

"I don't know," Sam said. "You might as well spend a few days at the beach, and then go back to the States. I don't even know where I am going from Aseania. I may just go on over to Hong Kong and then to Beijing while I'm out here."

"Okay," said Sally, cheerfully, though her tone of voice was exactly opposed to what she felt. "Take care of yourself."

But after he left, she still couldn't get it out of her head that he had had that glint in his eye. She thought she knew him well enough to recognize when he thought something was funny. But why was this funny? What was the matter with him?

The next day, Sam went to Torogi, wherever that was, and Sally went to the beach in the air-conditioned van thoughtfully provided by the hotel for its guests. The beach looked like the pictures on the front of a travel brochure: palm trees bending toward warm blue water, miles of clean golden sand, jungle-covered green mountains in the distance across the bay. It had gaily colored thatched roof cabanas and an excellent restaurant. The beach belonged to the hotel, and all any sun-bathing guest needed to do was wave a finger, and a waiter appeared at his side ready to take an order.

Sally put her belongings under a palm tree and headed across the broad strip of raked sand to the water. The sun was blistering, and the sand grew hotter and hotter under her feet until she ended up running. The water was very calm, and very warm, almost body temperature. It was also very shallow, and she waded out fifty yards before it was even deep enough to swim. Now her feet were not burning, but her shoulders and back were. She paddled around for a moment and waded back out. As she reached the water-line, she noticed several transparent objects that looked like plastic pillows lying on the wet sand. Jellyfish. Yecch.

Keeping a close eye on where she was stepping, she raced across the hot sand to her towel, spread it out in the shade of the palm, and lay down. The palm fronds rattled in a slight breeze and she looked up to see about five very large green coconuts directly overhead. She moved her towel out from under them, just in case, and lay down again. She fidgeted. Sally could not understand why anyone would want to spend fifteen minutes on a beach like this, much less days and days, as the other vacationers around her obviously were.

She stood, picked everything up, found the van, and hitched a ride back to the hotel.

There she asked at the desk how to get to Torogi.

The manager came out, looking anxious.

"We can't recommend that trip, madam. It is never done by tourists. There's nothing of interest to see there anyway."

"I don't care," said Sally. "I'm going. How do I get there?"

The manager sighed. "First you fly to Siyara, and then you take a bus from there."

"Please get me reservations on the next plane out, and reservations on a connecting bus," said Sally.

"Well, we can try on the plane, but the bus is first come, first served."

"Fine with me," said Sally, marveling that she didn't feel a single twinge of anxiety about this. Yet.

Kaki Besar, the domestic airline of Aseania, was one that even Marcy never heard of, Sally decided. It was rather novel to throw your own bag into the luggage compartment and climb up a ladder to get into the plane, which was a small two-engine DC-3 holding perhaps 30 passengers. It was even more novel to discover that she had only one end of the seat belt—the buckle end was missing. As the plane strained, roaring and shaking, at the end of the runway, prior to takeoff, Sally's seatmate flashed a gap-toothed grin at her, and said,

"Not worry. Velly safe airprane. Been frying since 1936."

They landed at Poro and Belait after flying over miles and miles of brilliant green rice paddies glinting in the sun. The first time the pilot swooped down and skimmed over the runway at about fifteen feet, Sally panicked. Then she saw the running animals beneath—water buffalo and goats and chickens—and realized that the pilot was only buzzing the runway to get the livestock off. They landed smoothly on the second pass. At Belait, it didn't bother Sally at all, and she was expecting something similar at Siyara, which was the next stop. Instead, at Siyara, which was in the mountains, the pilot flew straight at a cliff. The plane was bouncing and leaping in the air over great chasms with vicious clouds welling up out of them. Sally was just about to scream when

solid ground and a runway about a foot long appeared under the plane's wing, and they were down. The plane
stopped two feet short of the cliff face.

All the way, Sally felt good about her panic. It had been
normal human fear-of-crashing panic, not the old imaginary kind. Real risks, she was discovering, weren't nearly as
scary as imagined ones.

Sally climbed down, a bit rubbery legged, and waited for
the copilot—or somebody—to throw her bag down to her.
She was happy that she had had sense enough only to bring
her carryon after careful repacking. For she would have to
walk to the bus station, or so her seatmate had told her before he got off at Belait.

As she watched, the passengers for the return flight
boarded, the plane's engines, which had never stopped,
speeded up as it taxied to the cliff end of the short tilted
runway. Then it revved its engines until it seemed it would
shake apart, let go the brakes and roared down the runway.
At the end, it dropped off the cliff and disappeared from
sight. Sally's stomach turned over. Moments later the sturdy
little plane could be seen climbing steadily out of the chasm
into which it had flung itself.

Sally vowed not to fly out of Siyara, no matter what.

Siyara was a resort town high on the side of a mountain.
Sally had been told that this had once been a British hill
station, where the colonial and military officials came to
escape the lowland heat. And it did seem to Sally that it was
cooler here in the neat quiet pine-tree lined streets. She
walked along, hiking her bag, looking at the splendid views
of the flatlands below and the cloudy peaks above.

She bought some noodles from a street vendor, and putting her bag over her shoulder, went on her way, eating them
with the plastic fork the vendor gave her. They were delicious. She was actually enjoying herself. She was seizing the

day, whether or not Sam was around, whether or not Sam cared. It felt really good, she decided.

Sally began to notice that there were "natives" among the natives. They looked a little like lowland Aseanians, small and brown and black haired, but their features were different. And they did not wear the tropical uniform of chinos and loose shirt or simple dresses. The women wore gorgeously woven sarongs, cheap blouses or T-shirts and had snake skeletons braided into their hair. The men were not dressed so colorfully, but were tattoed from head to foot, and wore huge earrings and little pillbox hats on the side of their heads. And they walked with a waddling pigeon-toed gait.

"Wow," thought Sally. "Indians."

It was about two in the afternoon when Sally reached the bus station and found pandemonium. And Sam. Sally saw him sitting on a bench, looking slightly irritated. All around him milled the natives, all chattering away, smoking and spitting and petting the splendid fighting cocks on their arms. Sam, Sally thought, stuck out like a sore thumb. She sidled around where he wouldn't see and inquired at the station office and learned that not a single bus had left that day, due to a drivers' strike, which was just now settled. The bus for Torogi was about to leave, and she could just make it. The fare was twenty-two ringgits.

Sam, fortuitously, had disappeared, so Sally boarded. This bus had once been red, but was now so faded and battered and scratched that it looked like a patchwork quilt. Its engine chugged and groaned, and noxious black fumes billowed from its tailpipe. Two men stood on its roof, tying down luggage and bags of rice and bamboo cages of chickens. Inside, the seats were designed for small people, not tall Caucasians like Sally. They were also very hard, plastic over unpadded metal, patched with electrician's tape. Sally crammed herself into a window seat.

Then the other passengers began boarding. Sam was approximately the fifth person to board the bus. Hunched over because his head would hit the ceiling, he looked around the bus and saw Sally. There was a "clunk" as his head hit the roof in surprise—or perhaps shock. He walked down the aisle, holding his head with one hand and frowning.

"You'd better get off while you can," he said. "This is no trip for amateurs."

"Neither was the flight up," Sally said. "I thought that was a lot of fun. This will be even more fun."

"Sally, this is no place for you to be. I don't know what you're trying to prove, but this is no way to prove it. Go back to Kerida."

"You can't force me off this bus. I paid for my ticket. I'm going, whether you go or not. So just get used to that, and we'll get along fine. Why don't you sit down? I saved this seat for you." Sally patted the seat beside her. "Anyway, you're blocking the aisle."

Sam stowed his bag overhead and sat down. He rubbed the top of his head again. "Darn it, now I've got a knot on my head, and it's your fault."

"Nanny nanny boo boo," said Sally Forbes, age twenty-eight.

It was soon evident that the roof of the bus was loaded to capacity. More huge bags of rice were brought on board, great cardboard boxes of soap powder packets, of noodles, and the biggest bunch of garlic Sally had ever seen. And there was livestock: more chickens in cages, something that looked like a green pigeon, fighting cocks, and finally, a large pink pig and her six spotted piglets.

Two women with snake skeletons in their hair sat down in front of Sally and Sam. "What do they call themselves?" Sally asked. "They look like American Indians, only smaller. They must be relatives of mine."

"They're called Torogi, like the town," Sam told her. "Or vice versa. And you may be right. The latest theory is that they are more closely related to American Indians than to anyone else."

So Sally found herself behind the two Torogi women who were now smoking rolled-up green tobacco leaves and overhead in the rack were a carton of bottles of soy sauce and fish paste. The pig was tied to the leg of Sam's seat, sharing the aisle space with Sam's feet. The piglets were squealing and running under the seats.

The driver shifted gears and the bus gave a great groan and moved forward.

"How far is it to Torogi?" Sally asked.

"Sixty miles, maybe," Sam told her.

Not exactly comfortable, Sally thought, but if it was only sixty miles, two hours, she figured she could tough it out. She felt something pushing on her foot and looked down to see a piglet rooting at her shoe. The bus hit a pothole in the street, and there was a tremendous crash of metal, and Sally was bounced up so far that her head nearly hit the overhead rack. When she came back down there was a frightened squealing from the piglet. Sally wedged her knees up against the seat in front of her, picked up the piglet and held it on her lap. It calmed down immediately.

"You okay?" Sam asked, looking over at Sally. "This bus doesn't have any springs." That funny glint was back in his eyes, again.

"I noticed that," Sally said through gritted teeth.

One of the fighting cocks decided that it was sunrise and announced it. That set off all the other roosters aboard.

The pavement on the road ran out a mile out of town, and the road narrowed until it was a single narrow lane, full of large rocks, which the bus bounced over. The roosters gibbered and crowed at each crash. Sally learned how to brace herself, to protect her head, and to keep the piglet from his terrified squealing. He was nestled in her lap, contentedly grunting, while she acted as his shock absorber. Sam, she noticed, was having a better time of it. He was bigger; he could wedge himself in more firmly.

Soon they were bouncing and crashing along the side of a mountain, over a chasm. It seemed to Sally that the other side of the bus was scraping the mountainside, and that the wheels on her side were hanging over two thousand feet of empty air. This did not cause the driver to slow down. It did cause Sally to bow her head and close her eyes, so that she appeared to be praying. Appeared to be? She was. She shot a glance over at Sam. He was reading a paperback book, somehow.

She felt a tap on her shoulder and looked up. One of the Torogi women in the seat ahead had turned around and was grinning in a friendly manner. Her mouth appeared to be full of bright red blood. She said something and offered what appeared to be a small palm-leaf packet to Sally.

Sally took it and said, "Thank you."

The woman turned around. Sally said, "What is this?"

"Betel. You're supposed to chew it," Sam said. "Everyone else on the bus is." Sam's eye had that glint.

Then Sally saw that everyone was indeed chewing something and spitting red juice out the open bus windows.

"It's an appetite suppressant, and, I think, a mild narcotic," Sam said. "It also turns your teeth red."

"Well, it was nice of her to think of me," Sally said, putting the betel in her purse.

The road became narrower and steeper and rougher. Now little hills of water were pouring down the mountainside, running across the road, eating away big Vs. After what seemed hours, the bus chugged to a stop. The driver and his assistants, of whom there seemed to be eight or nine, all got out.

"What's happening?" Sally looked up for the first time.

Sam, who was taller, could see over the seats. "Looks like a landslide. Maybe we can't get through."

"What do we do then?"

"Back out, probably," Sam said laconically.

That time there was no gleam in his eye. Sally checked.

She tried not to imagine backing out. She decided that she and the piglet would walk out, rather than back out on this bus.

But the driver and his assistants got back on the bus, and the bus eased its way out onto a hill of gooey red mud. Very slowly, wheels spinning, it moved along and began to tilt. Sally made the mistake of looking out her window and now she really was looking straight down the chasm. The bus was still moving but was canted at a forty-five degree angle. Sally gripped the piglet with all her strength and closed her eyes.

The bus righted itself and ground on down the rocky road. Sally realized that somebody in the bus was screaming in fear and hoped it wasn't herself. Sam jogged her arm. "Stop squeezing that pig. Its mother is about to go after me."

Sally released the pig and looked over. The mother was indeed making ugly growling noises, fangs bared at Sam. Sally had never known that a pig had fangs or could growl. She handed the piglet, still whimpering, to Sam, who put it down beside its mother. Happy suckling sounds arose immediately.

After an hour of crashing, just when Sally thought she could brace herself no longer, the bus pulled to a stop. They were now nearly on top of a mountain, at very high altitude, and there was a bleak little village, or a scattering of shanties on the bald mountainside. There was also a shack with a sign that said "Ristoran."

"I wonder if we need reservations?" Sam said, waiting for the aisle to be cleared of people, cartons, pigs and rice bags.

The food was all out on display in the Ristoran. There was rice in a red sauce with chunks in it, rice in a brown sauce with chunks in it, and rice. There was orange soda and there were hard boiled eggs. Sally eyed the flies swarming over the exposed food and ordered three hard boiled eggs and a soda. There were some bananas, but one of the other passengers got all of them before Sally could ask.

"I'm having a wonderful time," said Sally. "This is so much fun."

"Me, too," said Sam.

Sally and Sam ate outside, standing up, exercising their legs. It was chilly, even cold, and very bleak and barren. The sun was very low in the sky.

"What do they do for a living, the people who live here?" Sally asked.

"I expect they were woodcutters. Until just a few years ago, this was all heavy rainforest."

"You're kidding," Sally gasped. "I haven't seen a tree since we started down this road."

"Unfortunately, it's true. The idea of conservation has never occurred to the folks in Kerida. Just exploitation. And it's not your relatives, the Torogi, who did it. It was the government and foreign logging companies. Or so my friend at the university said."

"How could anyone do that?" Sally asked, looking at the panorama of barren pale green peaks.

"It's easy," Sam said. "All you have to do is get a nice loan from an American bank. Or a bribe from a Japanese logging company."

"Did I detect a note of sarcasm there?" Sally said, looking at him closely.

He shook his head. "It's just facts. Only the facts, ma'am."

When they reloaded the bus in reverse order to the unloading, there were a few less people and cartons. But the pigs and the chickens and the rice bags were still with them. By now the sun was nearly down, and it was downright cold. Sally pulled the window closed and was glad the bus was so crowded. The people and the piglets would warm it up. She wondered where the people would spit their betel now the windows were closed.

As Sam settled into the seat beside her, getting his feet around the pig, she said, "We must be almost there. We've been on the road for four hours."

She had decided that she could take exactly one more hour of this. She felt black and blue all over, and her muscles ached from bracing herself for the bumps. She could feel the hard boiled eggs bobbing around in the soda in her stomach.

But Sam said, "I guess nobody told you. The schedule says it's a ten hour trip. We've got six hours to go. I'd suggest you try to sleep." Again the gleam. What was it?

"Sleep? Sleep?" Sally laughed and laughed, until she realized she sounded on the verge of hysterics. She managed to get it down to a giggle. "I think I'll wait until we get to the hotel." She stopped, suddenly sobered by a horrible thought. "If there *is* a hotel in Torogi, that is." She looked over at Sam, who was scratching the pig behind its ears.

"Oh, there's a hotel," Sam said. "But nobody in Siyara knew if it was open this time of year. But if it is, it's a wonderful bargain—four ringgits a night."

"Four ringgits a night? That's eighty-eight cents."

"See? It is a bargain," Sam said with that crooked grin.

Sally wedged herself even deeper into the uncomfortable seat and stared at the back of the seat in front of her. As the bus banged and bounced and clunked and chugged through the night, its single working headlight revealed only more and deeper chasms. Sally was happy she couldn't see a thing.

She did shoot an occasional sideways glance over at Sam. He seemed perfectly impassive, but it had begun to dawn on her that something was going on here that she didn't know about. That twinkle in his eye, for instance. Maybe he was...laughing at her? She thought about that for a moment and decided that it better not be true. Because she'd kill him with her bare hands if he was.

The only thing she said to Sam in the next six hours was, "Hand me that piglet, would you? He's awfully cute, and I promise not to squeeze him."

"That's okay. His mother and I are best friends, now," said Sam, who gave her the piglet—or its identical sextuplet. And then he jammed himself down further in the seat and promptly went to sleep.

Sally hugged the piglet and bared her teeth at Sam. But he was oblivious.

Chapter Eleven

Sally had to be carried off the bus with the rest of the cargo, but after a minute or two on solid ground, her legs began to work again and she was able to stagger to the hotel. It appeared to be open, and in the dark, it looked fine, if small. The sign over the door said, "Laird's Scottish Highland Manor." Inside was a very large room, with linoleum on the floor. Wooden tables and chairs were set in a regular dining room pattern before a long bar that had four dusty bottles on it.

Upstairs were the rooms. Sally dragged herself up the stairs behind the man, evidently the owner of the hotel, who was carrying the bags. Sam was behind her. There was a long hall with a curtain at the end and six doors leading off of it. The owner opened one of these doors and made a welcoming gesture at Sally. She stepped into her room.

It was spotlessly clean. The splintery wood floor looked polished. The single narrow bed held the whitest sheets she'd ever seen, though the most patched and darned. There was a single wooden chair and a bare lightbulb hanging from the ceiling. The window had screens and wooden louvers, but no glass. Everything but the floor and the lightbulb was painted white.

Never had anything looked so good to Sally. Until the owner of the hotel said, "Will Madam be wishing to have a shower this night?"

It was then that Sally realized her wish for a shower was greater than her wish to lie down on that clean white bed. She wanted a nice warm shower more than life itself. She ached all over and there was a distinct odor of piglet about her.

"Oh, that would be wonderful," she said.

"Then I shall prepare the shower," said the owner, bowing.

Sam was standing in the doorway. "Be careful with that shower. It may surprise you."

"Oh, shut up," Sally said. "Nothing would surprise me. I am truly a seasoned traveler."

And she closed the door in his face.

When the owner knocked politely on her door, Sally was ready, in her bathrobe, holding her towel and soap and shampoo. The owner led her past the curtain at the end of the hall. Behind it was a sink, and beside the sink was a table full of rum bottles.

"What's this for?" Sally asked.

"For shaving or for washing of the face or brushing of the teeth," he said. "The water for the sink is in the rum bottles."

"I see," said Sally.

The shower was in a closet-like room. It had a drain in the center of the floor. High on the wall was a contraption the like of which Sally had never seen. The owner explained that to operate the shower, one had only to stand under the showerhead and pull on the chain, thus. Sally nodded and closed the door.

She hung her bathrobe on a nail on the wall, and her towel on another, and put the shampoo and soap within easy reach. She looked down and inspected her body. She was somewhat startled to discover that she had no broken bones, no bruises, that all extremities were intact. Then she stood directly under the showerhead and reached out to pull the chain, anticipating the feel of deliciously hot water running over her everywhere, taking the ache and the exhaustion away.

She yanked on the chain and was inundated with icy water straight from the Antarctic. She let out a strangled shriek and let go of the chain. When the water stopped running down the drain she could have sworn she heard somebody laughing.

Gritting her teeth, she shampooed her hair, soaped her goose-bumped body, and stepped back under the shower. She held the chain for a good five minutes before she could bring herself to pull it. The soap was drying on her skin, cracking it, itching. It was, she thought, like giving the signal to fire to your own firing squad.

"One, two, three . . ." she said aloud. Then, "Four, five, six, seven, eight, nine, ten . . ."

"One, two, three, four, five . . . Oh, hell."

And so she pulled the chain.

After that, Sally knew anything else that she ever did in life would be easy. She could take any risk in the world. She was invincible.

On the way back, actually feeling pretty good, she kicked the door to Sam's room, and said, "Great shower. You ought to try it."

She climbed into the narrow little bed with the thin pillow and the patched white sheets. She closed her eyes, and as she had expected, she was back on the bus. She turned over on her face, gripped each side of the bedframe firmly so that she would not bounce out of bed, and fell immediately asleep.

When Sally woke up she hadn't the faintest idea of where she was. It was an all-white room, with a hard narrow bed, and with sun pouring through the louvered window. A hospital, perhaps? She shook her head and then it all came flooding back to her. She knew where she was—the ends of the earth. She lay back down and hoped it would go away. When it didn't, she flexed her arms and then her legs, remembering the bus trip. She wriggled her toes and her fingers. Everything worked, though a bit stiffly.

Finally she got out of bed and stretched. She felt all right. In fact, she felt good. She was feeling good about feeling good when she remembered the reason she was here: Sam Thatcher. Did she care that much about him that she'd go on with this? She stopped a minute and thought about that and then remembered that the only way out of here was on the bus, the same way they'd come in. She groaned.

Then she remembered some other things. Yes, she cared that much about Sam that she'd do these crazy things, and more. But not only that, she was interested in those dams. She, too, wanted to see these primitive tribal people here who would be displaced by them. She didn't like that lying prime minister in Kerida. Seize the day, she thought.

She jumped into jeans and an oversize and very wrinkled white shirt, and her red sneakers and went downstairs, saying a small prayer that hot black coffee was available in Torogi, Sulu Province, Aseania.

Coffee was indeed available, said the boy sweeping in the dining room. And so, she discovered, was Sam.

He was sitting at a rusty metal table on a kind of porch, drinking a bottle of beer. Sally slid into the chair opposite him. She was about to make a comment about the accommodations when she looked past him and said, instead, "Oh!"

The hotel and the town were at the bottom of a valley, and in front of Sally's eyes rose a steep wall of rugged mountain, crisscrossed with stone walls forming terraces. There were clusters of thatched huts and small stands of jungle dotting the mountain. From the top of the mountain a long lean waterfall gushed outward in stair-step leaps down to the river that ran through the town. Everything but the stone walls and the arching water was an unearthly green. That seven thousand feet of terraced mountain was utterly spectacular.

"Who did that? Those terraces?" Sally whispered, knowing she was looking at one of those extraordinary works of man, like the Great Wall of China or the pyramids.

"Fantastic, isn't it?" Sam said. "The Torogi did it. Took them about six thousand years. They did it all with their hands."

"But why?" Sally wondered.

"They needed to grow rice. Those are rice paddies. There's no flat land here."

Sally watched in awe as a Torogi woman carrying a huge bag of something on her head seemed to walk straight up the mountain.

"This afternoon, I have an appointment up there," Sam said, pointing at the highest cluster of thatched huts.

Sally looked. She could see no way up that mountain except climbing straight up.

"An appointment with whom?" she asked.

"The appointment is with the chief."

"I see."

"Don't let this go to your head," Sam said. "But I'd appreciate it if you came along."

Sally grinned. "You really want me to go? Think I can take it?"

"Maybe. The chief wants to meet you."

"Meet me?"

"Yep," said Sam. "You."

The boy brought a steaming cup of coffee and put a plate down on the table. "American breakfast," he said.

Sally looked at her plate. On it were two hard fried eggs, two toasted roof shingles and a small boiled potato.

"Thank you," she said. "That looks…wonderful." And compared to the hard boiled egg and soft drink of the night before, it was. She took a big sip of the coffee and began to feel almost in touch with reality again.

"How did you meet this chief to make the appointment?"

"I was up and out early this morning," Sam said, grinning that crooked grin. "I took a nice brisk shower and then I went to the market and started talking to people and I found a university student who speaks both English and Torogi. When he found out what I was interested in, he told me the first person I should talk to was the Datu because he was the most important person around. My friend in Kerida said the same thing. So I sent word to the chief, or Datu, that I was on my way. Bringing you."

"Okay. But how do we get there?" Sally asked, cutting into the potato. "I can't walk up that mountain the way those Torogi women do it."

"Never fear, there's a road. And we can hire a Jeep."

"With pigs?" said Sally.

"If you wish," said Sam. "We can hire some pigs, too."

* * *

The Jeep had climbed thousands of feet on a twisting rock-filled road beside a precipice and arrived at a saddle on top of the mountain. Sally and Sam had walked another mile along the tops of terrace walls, sometimes with abysses on both sides and found themselves in a cluster of huts. Each was on stilts and had a thatched roof that drooped so low over the wooden walls that these huts looked like pyramidal haystacks on stilts. Big-eyed naked children stared. Underneath each hut were stored agricultural implements, mostly wooden, and big clay jars, and beside each was a stone-lined hole in the ground containing fat, grunting spotlessly clean pigs.

"So you didn't need to bring your own, after all," Sam said to Sally, who was panting in the thin air and now on the verge of terminal vertigo.

The Datu came to greet them. Sally could see no sign that this was an important man, for he wore jeans, a T-shirt and running shoes. But she could see heavy tattoos on his arms.

"Welcome to my humble village, Mr. Thatcher and Miss Forbes. The women are preparing a small feast in your honor. You can smell the pig cooking. In the meantime, perhaps you would honor us by sharing a small libation, as our former British masters said."

His English was practically unaccented, Sally noticed, surprised. He ushered them up a ladder and into one of the huts. It was cool and dark under the thatch. In one corner Sally made out a woman, snake skeleton in her hair, dressed only in a brightly colored woven skirt, rocking a baby.

Sally fell through a black hole and landed in the pages of *National Geographic*. She had to look at Sam, big solid Sam, to make sure this was real. Sam must have known what she was thinking, because he winked. Sally felt better.

Sam leaned over and whispered, "Whatever he offers, drink it, no matter how horrible it is. Don't offend him." Sally felt worse.

"Have a seat," said the Datu, gesturing at a straw mat. Seating himself, he continued, "Usually when I have a guest who wishes to see our colorful tribal customs, I offer them our local drink, which is fermented rice wine and animal blood."

Sally's stomach churned. Sam put a gentle hand on her arm. She decided she would kill him, the very next chance she got. CPAs did not drink fermented rice and animal blood. Ever, under any circumstances, even when seizing the day.

"However, Miss Forbes, you need not have worried," said the Datu, with a small smile, which revealed teeth reddened by betel. "I only do that to tourists and anthropologists, which you are not. I have beer and I have a bottle of Scotch. Can I interest you in either?"

Sally pictured a green cloud of relief rising 30,000 feet over the little hut. "I'll have a beer," she said.

After everyone else had settled on beer, the Datu said, "I know what your first question is going to be. Where did I learn my English? I am a university graduate, in anthropology. The young man you ran into at the market is my son, who is currently attending university. We heard you were coming here, Mr. Thatcher, so we arranged for you to be here this afternoon."

"I am impressed," said Sam.

Sally looked closely at him. He was impressed. So was Sally.

"I know quite a bit about you, Mr. Thatcher. I know for instance, that you are a risk analyst. Is that not correct?"

Sam nodded.

Sally began to feel the hair on the back of her neck stand up. There was some vague foreboding in the air, if not in the Datu's voice.

"I also know that you are here about the hydroelectric project proposed by the government in Kerida," continued the Datu. His face, Sally decided, was pleasant, intelligent and totally inscrutable.

"That's also true," said Sam, warily, Sally thought.

"Well, Mr. Thatcher," the Datu said, " I want to tell you some of the risks involved. To put it bluntly, my people do not want those dams and we will use any means, fair or foul, to stop them."

Sally moved inadvertently closer to Sam.

"That's pretty unequivocal," Sam replied. "Why don't you want the dams? Though having seen the valley, I suspect I know."

"Obviously, the one proposed here will inundate the valley that has been the home of my people for six thousand years. The town would be gone, and half the rice terraces."

"And the other four dams?" Sam asked.

"All but one will destroy tribal homelands."

Sally felt sick. It sounded like the history of her mother's tribe.

"I believe the plan includes a proposal to resettle all the Torogi who are affected by the dams elsewhere. The trade-off is supposed to be electricity for millions as opposed to displacing a few thousand," said Sam.

"I wouldn't be too sure of that," said the Datu.

"Electricity for the millions may not quite be what they have in mind. We have reason to believe that most of the power will be diverted to a cellulose plant in Cagayan province. Having cut down all the timber here, they are going to start there. The plant, I believe, is to make cigarette filters, and it is owned by the Prime Minister and the Minister of Defense.''

"Can you prove that?"

"I will soon. My people in Kerida are tracing the financial interconnections now.''

"I heard something similar in Kerida myself,'' said Sam. "Go on.''

"Now I want to explain the risks.''

"Remember,'' said Sam, "I am a *financial* risk analyst.''

"I remember. The greatest financial risk would be to loan the money and never get the dams built at all, would it not?''

"That's true.''

"Do you know anything of our history, Mr. Thatcher? I mean the history of the Torogi?''

"Very little,'' said Sam.

"Our ancestors were here first. We are not even really related to lowland Aseanians. In fact, the Torogi are more closely related to Miss Forbes' people, the American Indians, or, as I believe you now call them, the Native Americans.''

"How did you know that?'' Sally almost squeaked.

"We have spies everywhere,'' said the Datu with a grin. "Actually, Mr. Thatcher told my son that. But to continue: we used to live in the lowlands, but many thousands of years ago we came to the mountains. The lowland was being invaded by different peoples, from whom we probably learned rice-growing. So we came here and began building our rice terraces, and for six or so thousand years nobody bothered us. Partly because we were so fierce that everyone who tried to come up here was prevented from doing so. We had a horrendous reputation. Even the British, who came here with guns, were afraid of us, and we held them off. When the rest of the country was a British colony, we were an island of independence within it, living by our old ways.''

"Hooray for you," said Sally.

"Alas, Miss Forbes—'' the Datu smiled his red smile ''—we had our U.S. cavalry, too. The Japanese in World War II. They were more implacable than we, and when the war was over, the lowlanders came in and we were just one more province, rich in timber and minerals, but otherwise the poorest people in the country.''

The Datu paused, then continued. "The new government sent in troops to enforce the laws that they made against us, and our ways were outlawed. Our mountains were clear-cut, our minerals strip-mined. Now they want to build dams in our ancestral valleys. The Torogi were completely demoralized after the war, but we had learned a few things from the Japanese. We have quietly reorganized ourselves in our old tribal patterns, we carefully saved the old ways and when the lowlanders and the multinationals left, having depleted our resources, we still had them. We also learned the ways of the lowlanders, and we took advantage of their educational system, to use it against them. Now we can fight them the old way, or their way, or anything in between.''

The Datu smiled again, this time at Sam. He lifted his arm, and the bare-breasted woman who had served the beer handed him a rolled-up piece of wovencloth.

"We are going to stop those dams, Mr. Thatcher," he said. He held up a ballpoint pen. "This is the new way: we will write everything from letters to the editor to publicity releases to environmental impact reports. And this is the old way...''

He unrolled the cloth. Inside was an ax, with an S-shaped beautifully decorated metal head.

"What's that?'' asked Sally with a sinking feeling.

"A head ax, Miss Forbes. The reason everyone for six thousand years was afraid of us. We haven't used these for some time, but we are prepared to use them again, if necessary. You see, Miss Forbes, we are headhunters."

Sally thought that for the first time in her life she was going to faint. She felt Sam's hand gripping her arm. Then she decided she was watching a movie, and the popcorn machine was giving off a distinct smell of barbecued pork.

With the head ax lying between them, the Datu looked at Sally and said, "Tell me, Miss Forbes, something about your tribal ways. I have never met a Native American before, and as an anthropologist, I find it a great treat. Our language has recently been discovered to be closely related to some Siberian languages, which in turn, are akin to those of the California coastal Indians. Is your language, perhaps, of the Iroquois group?"

Eventually, toward sundown, the pig was done, and everyone from the village gathered to watch it being carefully lifted from the pit and even more carefully carved. When everything was ready, Sally and Sam, seated on the right of the chief in a great circle, were served the first pieces with crisp skin on them in a spicy pinkish sauce. The women had cooked greens and rice, and everyone ate with gusto. Including Sally. It was the best food she'd had since leaving Kerida. And she was starved. She noticed Sam was eating heartily, too.

After that came the rice wine. And the dancing. And the music. The Datu, now wearing a headdress, leaned over to Sally and said, "We usually only do this for funerals or weddings, but I thought you'd like to see it, being a Native American."

Sally had been ashamed all day about her lack of knowledge about her own background. She began hoping that the Datu wouldn't ask her to demonstrate her own dances.

Then came more rice wine.

Sam leaned over and said to Sally, "Is this the equivalent of going to the Minister's private island or playing polo with the Minister of the Interior? Do you think they're trying to influence us?"

Sally whispered back, "No, I think the head ax was the attempt at influence."

Then she could have sworn the Datu winked at her. As if he had heard her. She figured he couldn't have. He was on the other side of her and there was that strange flute and drum music going.

Then came more rice wine.

Sally began to think it was pretty good.

Then from nowhere, the chief's son appeared. Unlike everyone else, except his father, he was dressed in jeans and T-shirt. The T-shirt had a picture of John Lennon on it. He had a guitar and he leaned on a black stone wall and started strumming it and singing. Very professionally, he introduced each song in English and explained it. The first two were traditional Torogi songs in English, his own translation. They were very haunting and simple and beautiful, Sally thought. Everyone applauded appreciatively when he finished.

More rice wine was served.

"Now I'll do a couple of Beatles songs," said the chief's son, and he did. There was even more applause.

Sally began to politely refuse more rice wine. So did Sam, she noticed. She wondered what he thought of all this. What she thought was that she'd somehow landed in a mountain-top nightclub, crossed with an anthropological museum. Especially when the chief's son said, "And now one of my own songs. This is about the dams and how the courageous Torogi stopped them. It is already being sung in the coffee-houses of Kerida. We have many allies, particularly among the students. Our cause is their cause.''

And he began to sing a song in Torogi that was so rous-ing that everyone was soon clapping and singing along. Sally was startled to hear the name of the Prime Minister in it, and the words "World Bank."

"This is the real attempt to influence," Sam said in her ear.

"Have you ever seen anything like this before?" Sally whispered. "I mean have you ever sat with headhunters and listened to protest songs before?"

Sam shook his head. "Can't say I have," he said.

"To tell the truth, I haven't either," Sally said and was happy to hear Sam chuckle.

"Are you having a good time?" he asked.

"The time of my life," Sally said, her foot tapping to the music. She looked at the smiling singing brown faces around her and then beyond them to the valley where the last of the evening sun was glinting off the rice terraces, making them glow like pools of molten gold stair-stepping down the steep mountain. She repeated, "The time of my life."

Sam put a hand on her shoulder and grinned. "Me, too, Pocahontas."

Sally was suddenly full of joy.

When it was too dark to see, lanterns were brought out, and though the music continued, Sam pointed out that they'd best be getting back to town. Everyone shook hands all around, invitations to visit were passed back and forth, farewells said, and the chief himself, carrying a kerosene lantern, led them the precipitous way back to the Jeep. It was tricky in the dark, but not as bad as daylight, Sally thought. At least in the dark you couldn't see the drop-off as you jumped from slippery black rock to slippery black rock along the tops of the walls holding up the terraces.

Once they reached the Jeep, the Datu said, "I am sure you'll make the right recommendation, Mr. Thatcher. I have no doubt of that. And Miss Forbes, you know you are especially welcome here any time. We must figure out what our degree of relationship is."

Sally and Sam climbed into the Jeep. Sam started the Jeep, put it in first gear, and turning on the headlights, began the long slow grind down the mountain. After the second turn, the motor died. Sam swore and slammed on the brakes. He tried to start it. No luck. He checked the gas tank with a stick. Half full. Sally began looking for a flashlight. There was none, but she did find a box of kitchen matches, and Sam tried to fix the engine while Sally lit match after match so that he could see. No luck at all.

"Now what, Pocahontas?" he said.

"Well, heck," said Sally, "Why don't we just walk back up to the Datu's place and ask him if he's got an extra hut or something."

In the pale starlight, Sally was laughing.

"Why are you laughing?" Sam asked. "This is a serious situation. We are stranded on top of a mountain clear to hell and gone with only a bunch of headhunters to ask for help."

"I think it's great," said Sally.

"That's my girl," said Sam, grabbing her and kissing her as hard as he could without falling off the narrow road. In Sally's head the skyrockets began, and in her heart there grew a commensurate warmth that went beyond mere desire and into something so elemental and all encompassing that she felt that her physical substance had disappeared and combined with the warm solid real person that was Sam. When they were out of breath and starry-eyed and weak,

Sam came up for air and said, "You haven't reverted to CPA for three whole days, you know. I think you're cured."

"I know I'm cured," Sally said, hugging him as hard as she could. "This is great. I can't wait to tell Alicia about it. She'll never believe it. I'm stranded at the end of the earth and I love it."

"Alicia already has a pretty good idea, I expect," said Sam. "When I talked to her, she said she thought you had it in you."

"When did you talk to Alicia?" asked Sally, leaning back in his arms and looking up at him with narrowed eyes.

"Several times," said Sam. "She was a big help. It was her idea to let you think you were following me."

"It was what? It was what?" Sally was now agitated.

"You heard me, Pocahontas."

"You mean you knew I'd end up here? I was manipulated?"

"Manipulated isn't the right word. Alicia insisted that if I said 'no you couldn't come', you'd do it. She was right."

Sally backed off out of his arms, edging carefully past the lifeless Jeep. "So that was a test? Were you laughing at me?"

"Not very much," said Sam. "In fact, not at all. Except maybe for the shower."

"Did you know how rough that trip was going to be? That plane flight and that bus ride?"

"Yes and no. I knew it would be bad, but I didn't know it would be terrible."

"Tell me why I shouldn't throw rocks at you and walk back to town," Sally said. "I should be really angry at you."

"But you're not?"

"No, I'm not."

"What are you, then," said Sam taking her in his arms again.

Sally cuddled up next to his chest and looked up at him in the starlight. "In love, I guess."

"I'll settle for that," said Sam.

There was another silence while they explored that idea.

"How does this strike you for reality," said Sam. "Is it real or unreal?"

Sally looked out over the dark valley. In the starlight she could make out the terraces climbing upward, the river flowing silver at the bottom, the waterfall leaping. Here and there were flickering orange lights, which marked the lantern-lit tribal huts.

"It's real," said Sally. "And it's even perfect. And Holy Island was real. It was the rest of it that wasn't. I was just confused. But not any more."

So they climbed back up and teetered across the terraces back to the village where the singing and dancing was still going full blast. The Datu did indeed have an extra hut, a kind of ceremonial place, and gave them blankets and sleeping mats. But it was far too early to sleep, or even retire to the hut away from the curious eyes of the village.

They went back to the party, but were unable to concentrate on the singing. They just kept staring at each other. It was kind of embarrassing, Sally thought, but what did she care? She was particularly embarrassed when an old crone went up to the Datu and whispered something very emphatically, pointing at her and Sam. The Datu said something in reply, the crone said something, and the Datu nodded.

Then he came over to them.

"Miss Forbes, Mr. Thatcher, this is quite a delicate subject, but the oldest woman in the village, and therefore the most revered and the judge of manners and morals, is rather indignant. You see, the ceremonial hut is for ceremonies:

funerals, weddings, rites of passage. She does not feel it is proper for an unmarried couple to use it. I am afraid that one or the other of you will have to sleep somewhere else.''

"I see," said Sam. "Well, we'll have to respect that."

Oh, dear, thought Sally.

"There is an alternative," said the Datu. "It's obvious to everyone that the two of you are—well, as you Westerners would put it, crazy about each other. Why don't we marry you two? In a tribal ceremony? That would satisfy everyone, including my aunt, the one who is mad at me for using the ceremonial hut as a hotel room. Of course, it's a little backward. The ceremony usually comes first, and then the feast. But since we've finished the feast . . ."

"Okay," said Sam, conversationally, as if he were accepting the offer of another beer. "That would be nice."

"What?" said Sally. "Wait, Datu, can we have a few minutes to talk this over?"

"Certainly," said the Datu, returning to his place of honor in the circle.

Sally waited until he was out of earshot and said, "Sam, he's serious. And if we go through with this, we should take it seriously. Otherwise we'd be making fun of them. I thought you were more sensitive than that."

"I *am* serious," said Sam. "I want to get married."

"I'm happy to hear it," Sally said, "but who is the lucky bride?"

"Oh, I forgot," said Sam. "Will you marry me?"

Sally had the last momentary panic attack of her entire life. "What about the house you're buying? What about my job, what about the IRS?"

"Marry me, no questions asked?"

"I'll marry you," said Sally. "No questions asked."

"Okay, Sacajawea, let's go."

* * *

The ceremony was brief but colorful. Sally was dressed up by the women in full regalia, snake skeleton in her hair, bare breasts and all, but at the last minute they allowed her to wear a T-shirt. A plain one. Sam wore the clothes he had on, plus the hat tilted over one ear. He politely refused the offer of a tattoo on his throat, pleading lack of time.

The entire ceremony was in the Torogi language and involved a lot of talk among the men before the bride was brought out. It seemed to center on rice. Rice, rice wine, rice straw, green rice shoots, and of course the benign spirits of the rice, all of them promising fertility and growth. Sally poured rice wine at Sam's feet, and he poured rice wine at her feet. Various tribespeople gave them gifts, mostly of rice and a few pots. The Datu said a few words in Torogi, and then, with a grin, he said, "I now pronounce you man and wife."

And then there was more rice wine.

It was well after midnight when Sam and Sally retired to the ceremonial hut. The old crone listened outside for a while until satisfied that things were going right, and then she, too, retired.

"She's a Torogi Mrs. Musgrove," Sally whispered.

"She's gone," said Sam, peeking out the door. "Finally."

But Sally said, "Wait. Now I get to ask questions. What are you going to recommend about the dams?"

Sam sighed. "What do you think? Would you mind taking that snake thing out of your hair?"

"To put it in your terms, I'd say that based on the Datu alone, there is zero chance those dams will ever be built in the next thousand years."

"Very good. I may even make you a partner. Now take off that T-shirt, before I rip it off."

"Another question. What are my chances of getting to go on the next trip—anywhere?"

"A hundred percent," said Sam. "Now that silly skirt. I can't figure out how to untie the belt."

"Another question," said Sally. "Where can I find a phone? I've got to call the office. I forgot that I told that new CPA to come in Monday and I won't be there."

"Damn the new CPA," said Sam. "Anyway, there isn't a single telephone in the whole province. You can't call out."

"And nobody can call in, right?"

"Right," said Sam. "Ummmm. Do that again."

"So we can stay here for a while," said Sally. "With no interruptions."

"No interruptions. Come here, Pocahontas."

"Mrs. Pocahontas," said Sally.

"Mrs. Pocahontas," said Sam. "Ummmm."

"I never want to leave," breathed Sally.

"Why?" said Sam.

"I keep thinking about that bus ride and that airplane," Sally told him. "Is there another way out of here?"

"No," said Sam, sounding slightly pained. "Is that the only reason you want to stay?"

"No. Let me show you the real reason I want to stay."
Short silence.

"That's a good reason," said Sam. "Show me again."
Long silence.

"Sam? Are we really married?"

"Till death do us part, Sacajawea."

"Are you healthy?" Sally asked.

"Very healthy," said Sam. "How about you?"

"Oh, I'm very healthy, too."

"Then there's a hundred percent chance we'll live happily forever after."

"I'll take that risk," said Sally.

Sally was very, very happy. Sam didn't realize it, but she was still a CPA. She knew the great bottom line when she saw it.

*   *   *   *   *

Take 4 bestselling love stories FREE

Plus get a FREE surprise gift!

PASSPORT TO ROMANCE
SWEEPSTAKES RULES

1. **HOW TO ENTER:** To enter, you must be the age of majority and complete the official entry form, or print your name, address, telephone number and age on a plain piece of paper and mail to: Passport to Romance, P.O. Box 9056, Buffalo, NY 14269-9056. No mechanically reproduced entries accepted.

2. All entries must be received by the CONTEST CLOSING DATE, DECEMBER 31, 1990 TO BE ELIGIBLE.

3. **THE PRIZES:** There will be ten (10) Grand Prizes awarded, each consisting of a choice of a trip for two people from the following list:
    i)   London, England (approximate retail value $5,050 U.S.)
    ii) England, Wales and Scotland (approximate retail value $6,400 U.S.)
    iii) Carribean Cruise (approximate retail value $7,300 U.S.)
    iv) Hawaii (approximate retail value $9,550 U.S.)
    v)   Greek Island Cruise in the Mediterranean (approximate retail value $12,250 U.S.)
    vi) France (approximate retail value $7,300 U.S.)

4. Any winner may choose to receive any trip or a cash alternative prize of $5,000.00 U.S. in lieu of the trip.

5. **GENERAL RULES:** Odds of winning depend on number of entries received.

6. A random draw will be made by Nielsen Promotion Services, an independent judging organization, on January 29, 1991, in Buffalo, NY, at 11:30 a.m. from all eligible entries received on or before the Contest Closing Date.

7. Any Canadian entrants who are selected must correctly answer a time-limited, mathematical skill-testing question in order to win.

8. Full contest rules may be obtained by sending a stamped, self-addressed envelope to: "Passport to Romance Rules Request", P.O. Box 9998, Saint John, New Brunswick, Canada E2L 4N4.

9. Quebec residents may submit any litigation respecting the conduct and awarding of a prize in this contest to the Régie des loteries et courses du Québec.

10. Payment of taxes other than air and hotel taxes is the sole responsibility of the winner.

11. Void where prohibited by law.

COUPON BOOKLET OFFER TERMS

To receive your Free travel-savings coupon booklets, complete the mail-in Offer Certificate on the preceeding page, including the necessary number of proofs-of-purchase, and mail to: Passport to Romance, P.O. Box 9057, Buffalo, NY 14269-9057. The coupon booklets include savings on travel-related products such as car rentals, hotels, cruises, flowers and restaurants. Some restrictions apply. The offer is available in the United States and Canada. Requests must be postmarked by January 25, 1991. Only proofs-of-purchase from specially marked "Passport to Romance" Harlequin® or Silhouette® books will be accepted. The offer certificate must accompany your request and may not be reproduced in any manner. Offer void where prohibited or restricted by law. LIMIT FOUR COUPON BOOKLETS PER NAME, FAMILY, GROUP, ORGANIZATION OR ADDRESS. Please allow up to 8 weeks after receipt of order for shipment. Enter quickly as quantities are limited. Unfulfilled mail-in offer requests will receive free Harlequin® or Silhouette® books (not previously available in retail stores), in quantities equal to the number of proofs-of-purchase required for Levels One to Four, as applicable.

OFFICIAL SWEEPSTAKES
ENTRY FORM

Complete and return this Entry Form immediately—the more Entry Forms you submit, the better your chances of winning!
- Entry Forms must be received by **December 31, 1990**
- A random draw will take place on **January 29, 1991**
- Trip must be taken by **December 31, 1991**

3-SR-3-SW

YES, I want to win a PASSPORT TO ROMANCE vacation for two! I understand the prize includes round-trip air fare, accommodation and a daily spending allowance.

Name_____

Address_____

City_____ State_____ Zip_____

Telephone Number_____ Age_____

Return entries to: **PASSPORT TO ROMANCE**, P.O. Box 9056, Buffalo, NY 14269-9056

© 1990 Harlequin Enterprises Limited

COUPON BOOKLET/OFFER CERTIFICATE

Item	LEVEL ONE Booklet 1	LEVEL TWO Booklet 1 & 2	LEVEL THREE Booklet 1, 2 & 3	LEVEL FOUR Booklet 1, 2, 3 & 4
Booklet 1 = $100+	$100+	$100+	$100+	$100+
Booklet 2 = $200+		$200+	$200+	$200+
Booklet 3 = $300+			$300+	$300+
Booklet 4 = $400+	____	____	____	$400+
Approximate Total Value of Savings	$100+	$300+	$600+	$1,000+
# of Proofs of Purchase Required	4	6	12	18
Check One	____	____	____	____

Name_____

Address_____

City_____ State_____ Zip_____

Return Offer Certificates to: **PASSPORT TO ROMANCE**, P.O. Box 9057, Buffalo, NY 14269-9057

Requests must be postmarked by **January 25, 1991**

- ✂ - - - - - -

 ONE PROOF OF PURCHASE

3-SR-3

To collect your free coupon booklet you must include the necessary number of proofs-of-purchase with a properly completed Offer Certificate

© 1990 Harlequin Enterprises Limited

See previous page for details